Praise for Maawaam's Shadow Book...

"In *My Shadow Book* Jordan Rothacker is amanuensis to a mysterious yet familiar intelligence, and is our guide to a literary operation where—between the fragments, aphorisms, and stories—we are reflected in his gleaming scalpel. Part autopsy, part reconstruction, a stitched maze, here is the melancholy play of Borges, delighting along the seam between Boswell and Roswell. Rothacker's shadow men maintain an Area 51 of style and secrets. Recognize yourself there, or discover yourself there, the joy of *this* shadow book is in its devotion to the personal canonical, to discovering alien knowledge, the voices, zones, and memories that preserve us."

- James Reich, author of *Mistah Kurtz* and *Soft Invasions*

"In *My Shadow Book,* by Maawaam, editor and writer Jordan A. Rothacker weaves a tapestry of symbiotic diary entries, sections of prose, drawings, and dark musings from a dark and light soul who seems to teeter along the precipice of falling into eternal gray shadows. If the writer Maawaam is a word tour guide through existential angst and evanescent clarity then Rothacker is the hidden conductor, keeping time to his haunting song. Like ink dripping from a gothic paintbrush, text varies from expertly relayed metaphor to psychological realism. In one section Maawaam decrees: 'We bring out this army of bricks and stones and build this city...protecting truth, it moves from tower to tower,' and in the next, this modern seeming sage bemoans: 'I wish I could just walk into to the light, live in the light. I wish I could just give up the ghost.' Readers can be grateful that Maawaam keeps his ghosts close; we feel them on every page."

- Jennifer MacBain-Stephens, author of *Your Best Asset is a White Lace Dress* and *The Messenger is Already Dead*

Praise for the Rothacker's earlier work...

"Any book blurb serves two functions: (1) Contextualizing of a work. (2) The lending of authorial imprimatur. *And Wind Will Wash Away* is too huge, too sprawling, too complex, too interesting and too weird for pithy contextualization. So here's what I'll say: I really, really, like this book."

- Jarett Kobek, author of *I Hate the Internet*, *ATTA*, and *The Future Won't Be Long*

"Jordan A. Rothacker's Atlanta operates in a nebulous place, shifting between this world and one in which the object of one's faith is almost close enough to touch. [In *And Wind Will Wash Away*] Detective Jonathan Wind explores this place as an observer, not a participant, head and heart kept at bay in all things—in faith, in love. Rothacker's scholarly and lyrical prose is something for the reader to grab ahold of as we follow Jonathan Wind. With Wind, we learn. Perhaps, too, we believe."

- Pam Jones, author of *The Biggest Little Bird*

"You'd be hard-pressed to find a more literary, erudite and metaphysical noir novel than the one now in your hands [*And Wind Will Wash Away*]. Detective Jonathan Wind's search for the killer of his beloved mistress, Flora Ross, leads him through history, literature, art, and an Atlanta that swirls with ghosts, tricksters, demons, saints and a phantasmagorical array of urban characters you haven't seen since Fellini filmed his dreams and nightmares of Rome."

- Reginald McKnight, author of *White Boys* and *He Sleeps*

"Part farce, part gumshoe noir, part deep inquiry into the nature of belief—*And Wind Will Wash Away* is all of these things and more. Under Jordan Rothacker's pen, the American South is rendered an absurd and mystical topography that brings to mind such writers as Thomas Pynchon, James Purdy, David Foster Wallace, William S. Burroughs, and David Lynch. Be prepared for a crazy, inspired, breathtaking ride."

- Christian Kiefer, author of *One Day Soon Time Will Have No Place Left to Hide*

"Rothacker has seamlessly sewn together detective fiction, gritty Beat literature, and serious theological speculation in his debut novel. *And Wind Will Wash Away* is at once erudite and entertaining, and Rothacker depicts the city of Atlanta with a knowing intimacy that reminds me of Jean-Paul Sartre describing Paris or John O'Hara describing New York City. The characters, the ideas, and the setting are all alive and utterly themselves in this impressive work of philosophical fiction. Get a copy for yourself and one for a friend, because you're going to want to talk about this book for a long time to come."

- Okla Elliott, author of *From the Crooked Timber* and *The Doors You Mark Are Your Own*

My Shadow Book

By
MAAWAAM

MY SHADOW BOOK

*(Tales of the Shadow Men,
Selected from the Notebooks
of One of Their Own)*

By
MAAWAAM

Edited By
Jordan A. Rothacker

Denver, Colorado

Published in the United States by:
Spaceboy Books LLC
1627 Vine Street
Denver, CO 80206
www.readspaceboy.com

First printed October 2017

ISBN-10: 0-9987120-5-1

ISBN-13: 978-0-9987120-5-5

Editor's Preface:

In the summer of 2011 I discovered Maawaam's being in a box. The form his being took in that box was in journals, scraps of paper, scribbled on leaves, photographs, and drawings. The journals were the most significant abundance of being. For the last six years I have studied his being in the form I found it. The work you hold is a disservice to being, but what I hope is a service to the world because the being of Maawaam is worth beholding. My crime is that of order; from the gods I have stolen form and given it to Maawaam, the being. I have put his writings into his journals where they fit chronologically and evidentially. I have found what I believe to be the thread of development toward being from box to book. My worry is that as the form becomes the being dies.

It has been an honor and burden to behold these texts. Like Brod to Kafka, I have felt a duty to this writer to give his work to the world, even against his wishes. Laborious hours I have spent enrapt and even subdued by the hundreds of pages of hand-written journals, with my eyes given respite at times by the typed pages taped within. Moreover, Maawaam is a self-proclaimed traitor to his order. Maawaam names names. Where is my culpability? My simple belief is that the world needs to know the secrets that Maawaam has kept. Sheltered in truth, I await and accept the consequences.

I have served my function as editor to not only reduce the original bulk down to a manageable whole, but also one that flows through a progression toward understanding this character as he comes to understand himself. These are his own writings and the question of their veracity—and the veracity of the Shadowmen—is now in your hands. I have valued them as simply what they are: prose, thoughts, and a life; as incomplete and shadowy as any will ever truly appear.

As once said one of the Shadowmen mentioned here within:

Camerado, this is no book,
Who touches this touches a man

The Shadow Man said I could follow him. I told him I had been in the light for too long. There was still time, he said. I could step beyond the sun.

He took out his notebook. A black notebook emblazoned with a black sun, gray shading around the sun's points, demarcating it through bright shadow. He made notes while he was looking at me like he was doing a blind contour drawing. Eventually I would learn to write this way. Write without looking away, write without thinking, write like it was my job, my calling, my duty. And it was. Like a blind contour drawing.

The swastika is an ancient black sun. It belonged to everyone. The Nazis appropriated it. They knew of us. They thought they were Shadow Men. They were wrong. Horribly wrong.

In the city each building is a pregnant Angel. They wave and bend, fecund with half-men, half-divines. They make only heroes, but born into the city, walking in their shadows we all lose our pedigree.

To the untrained eye, each building is a tombstone. They read epigraphs in the windows, they see block letters, lit up at night, in the deep eyes of the Angels, Angel teeth, Angel smiles, Angel navels, Angel birth canals, Angel anuses. They take everything, everywhere, for pleasure, and for breeding, people of the city, half-gods.

The black star is a black sun. For the Shadow Men in

other systems and galaxies there is always the burning center to obscure and harness. Always light and always shadow. Always the space between, liminal, interstitial, bardo. This is where we work. Our God Janus. Our month January. Looking forward into the light of the future. Looking back into the light of the past. The present is shadow.

Every code and mode is open to a Shadow Man. Mao suspected our existence and copped some of our methods describing the basic guerrilla strategy as one that "must be adjusted to the enemy situation, the terrain, the existing lines of communication, the relative strengths, the weather, and the situation of the people." That's what we do.

Shadow Women are the strongest of us.

Over time the name Shadow Men found prevalence, but women have always made up more than half our ranks, often the best of us. They have always retained the ghost the longest and for this reason many have suffered free from posterity.

Oh Anna Kavan,
Oh Sister Anna, a Shade born and a Shade to her grave.

She did her work, our work, by means exceptional and painful...

The people of the sun are exceptionally cruel to women, which makes all of our work more important. She adapted to walk in the light by finding her secret name, her *nom de guerre*, and armed with a fucking bazooka she fought to the end.

She was always baiting, teasing out the ghost, and trying to walk in the light as shadowed as possible. She began one of her greatest short stories thusly:

> *The new, the great, the divine star is like to other. It alone has the glory, the godlike power to create new forms of life and a world of its own... Now the star is man's new god, producing changes unprecedented in his planetary environment, setting in motion undreamed of chains of events, destroying delicate balances which took milleniums to evolve.*

When we meet in bardo, it is always her garden and always replete with loaded bazookas.

"Real life is a hateful and tiresome dream," wrote Sister Kavan.

We were in the class of scribes during the dynasties of Ancient Egypt (lest we forget Brother Thoth) and we have served as shaman on the tundra of Siberia.

Brother Burroughs has always been one of my closest guides when I stepped out of the light. Early on he taught me that, "All techniques fall short of the artist's impossible objective. All serious art attempts the impossible. If art became too precise it could kill, because it could evoke any emotion in the reader or viewer. All serious and dedicated artists attempt the miraculous: the creation of life."

By the time I was in the shadows I understood what he meant when he said that we must dream for others, that we must dream out loud for them, even if they don't seem to hear us. In the bardo he once told me, "You see, and everything you see is alive, and everything you see means something special to you because *you* see it. If it meant nothing to you, you wouldn't see it."

From him I learned to see, as I also learned to write. Here in my little dark notebook I do my little dark work, our work.

Sister Sylvia sang my soul so sweetly in her short story where she tried so hard to give up the ghost, our ghost. For a formative time I made for my bible her book of stories and fragments. I wanted to become Johnny Panic and I wanted to be the medium of dreams.

Sometimes when I wake up in the morning, there is a glass of warm milk upon my nightstand she has left for me. Is she my sister-mother-lover-friend? Sure, but mostly she is my comrade.

Shadow Men speak to each other over time, in image, page or edifice. We have our ways, and we have *all* ways.

Occasionally, in working to serve the people of the sun, we try to give it all up to them. A game we play.

"Giving up the ghost" we call it.

The "ghost of a chance."

Many angels live in the shadows. Recording Angels, the easiest, Didactic Angels, the most difficult job. Why else record, but to teach? How else to teach, without knowing?

For many it is fun to tease out the ghost: "An observer is a prince who is everywhere in possession of his incognito," one of our most noble brothers, Baudelaire, gave up. He said prince, I say angel, and either way no one ever knew what he was really talking about.

Brother Benjamin added to this, as we do for each other over time: "In times of terror, when everyone is some sort of conspirator, everybody will be in a position of having to play detective."

They never understand us, but we don't work for the recognition.

THIS IS A
TIME OF TERROR.

There is no debate, even with the oldest and most learned of us—awake and aware—that E.A. Poe was one of us. He was flawed as we all are, half-divine, broken deep inside.

Our world is lonely, even though we are all together, all the time, across time. He teased out the ghost so much, he wanted so dearly, drunkenly, to give it up. His "Man in the Crowd" is the saddest expression of this ghost.

She woke just after me and next to me. She is beautiful.

What is the weather like, she asked.

I don't know, I told her. I had yet to do my scouting on the day. All my preparedness went into a night with her, all my attention.

It sounds sunny, she said.

Oh? I smiled.

I hear yardwork, or a distant machine for yardwork, maybe a sprinkler. It sounds like there are people out in the sun, it sounds sunny.

I smiled. I was suspicious of her words, and her insight, but they drew me to her. I never sleep this late, but it looked like I wasn't going to leave this bed for a while.

Did I always know I was a Shadow Man, that this was my destiny? I am too realistic and humble to say yes, but there were clues.

Once during my last year of college, I had a dream that I had gone to a special lecture. It was at a university that did not resemble my own. I don't remember the lecture, just standing on the stairs outside the hall talking about it after. What the lecturer revealed, his findings, was that through crazy math and an amazing telescope, and maybe some celestial geometry, he could tell that from the perspective of the Andromeda Galaxy our planet was one of the three points of Orion's Belt. Orion's Belt from their perspective of the constellation.

The whole universe seemed frightfully small and knowable to me. I woke in a sweaty panic. From a fever dream I beheld a glimpse of my place in the universe and the network of connections was crushing.

From a different dream during my first year of college I wrote this beginning of a short story. The story will never be finished. This fragment is all there is. Such is life. Years later I tacked on an epigraph. Such is life.

Mornings Endings

"Caesar speaks of Dis, the lord of the Underworld, as the ancestral god of the Gauls. For this reason, Caesar says, the Gauls count each day as beginning with the preceding night."--Prudence Jones and Nigel Pennick, *A History of Pagan Europe*

Waking up this morning I had to sweep up shattered remains of a dream. I can't remember well, but in some parts of it it seemed like I was back at my old college. I remember very clearly a fight between Punk Dave and Bible Dave except in the dream they seemed to be switched, Punk Dave was trying to get everyone to join his cult and Bible Dave hated everyone. That was in one room. Next I was in another room and someone I thought was my girlfriend was there and she was sprawled on a table of what seemed a bar and wanted me to give it to her. When I looked at my crotch it seemed that I had to fuck her with this apparatus that looked like a big government carrot, all rigid and plasticy, the kind they build to replace the unpredictable natural ones. When the girlfriend saw my sour contortions she said, "Don't worry. It's made in America, just like everybody!" My body ran from her down a hall covering ground quicker than I could turn my head and acknowledge. There was someone behind me. I sprinted up a short flight of stairs. He reached for the banister as I hopped over it. I saw it happen in slow motion, he grabbed my ass. I landed and he turned and giggled. He had the hat and belt of a frat boy. I ran on. I saw a door. I heard the alarm. I heard my mother. I was out.

I woke uncomfortably and sweaty. My arms bore finger marks as if I held on very tight as I slept. My boxers were moist. They stuck to my belly. The morning smelt dank like fresh holocaust. Yes, this I could tell as I dragged a couple of eye-crunchies down my cheeks from their lodgings. To begin this day was the choice I appeared to have. I rose and began the dressing process. Khakis make a man out of a boy, so they seemed the appropriate choice. Choosing a shirt to match my khakis wasn't hard, all my shirts match my khakis. Shoes are incidental and black is universal. Sox are never seen. I grabbed my jacket and went down to my mother. Delightfully, the breakfast she lovingly prepared was exactly the same as yesterday's. Oh, except this time she used spices. She means well. Satiated, I stood, collected my things, and said goodbye to my mother. Satiated, I was out.

FEVER DREAM

I'm touching the sun,
of a different world,
behind your eyes

There are those nights when you get up to go the bathroom—she remains there asleep—and you catch your reflection and you can see he is dying and you feel like you're dying and you can feel it, the dying slowly and you wonder, is this how everyone feels all the time?

Steps of stone, lined with steel, descending, cutting right, around the building they curve with angles, so many perfect triangles. When you start you are above the bridge. When you end you are below the bridge around the corner.

You never touch the bridge. Only the city can do this.

She accepts my secrecy, believing it all done in the service of my art. She likes that I am a writer. There is a cache for her, dating a writer. More than my day job.

It has always been an easy cover for a Shadow Man, since its part of what we do anyway. The ones who have received fame have had great difficulty, but everything is difficult for us anyway.

This line of thought brings out my "anyway." Ours is a lonely life and relationships are difficult. The cover helps, but I should produce something before the cache goes stale for her and she leaves. But they all leave sometime. Anyway...

"Plagiarism is necessary. It is implied in the idea of progress. It clasps the author's sentence tight, uses his expressions, eliminates a false idea, replaces it with a

right idea."
I wrote that.

Sister Acker launched assaults on letters, and worked in the light, in the system, to fuck the system, bending narratives and words until they break and reassembling from the shards, her way, our way, the toxic patriarchy of the people of the sun where in fear everything is binary, everything is this/or, everything is fearful Otherness. But in these charcoal gray shadows, we funnel light, reclaiming it, piratically.

Every Shadow Man is for his time. Each today is for this one; all of my predecessors were for their own.
In this time, in this now, right now, I have a

visual mantra. I shut my eyes and see the final scene from the film *Fight Club*. The buildings are raised and go down, the terror and abuses have the chance to finally end. It is a visual mantra, a postcard of hope. "Wish You Were Here!" it reads, a greeting from a paradisiacal land. You could be here too! The guitar of Joey Santiago rings out with its loud creaky harmony notes.

The back of the postcard reads:

"We gotta get it together again, like the motherfucking Weathermen."

"You don't need to be a weatherman to know which way the wind blows."

"I need vengeance like a tired man needs a bath."

As each Shadow Man and Woman are for their respective places and times, sometimes I visit Brother Santoka Teneda, one hundred years ago wandering the Japanese countryside. He's seen so much sadness, death, and life. He found peace, and he found peace in his work. He walked, he drank sake, and he wrote haiku. His work was complete and it still comforts me:

> Working,
> And Working harder;
> Still the pampas grass grows.

AND

> I've something to eat
> And something to make me drunk;
> Rain in the weeds.

Mirrors are our best friends.
The City is a mirror.
The wilderness may be an echo chamber, but the city is a mirror.
We see you in everything. In every puddle, in every storefront, in every rearview.

We read you backwards and know you forward. Each adjust of the bra strap, pick of the nose, petty theft, look of disgust or lust, are all reflected, and read. You are known by us, because you want to be.

Every mirror is naked.

244. The doors and windows of a house are replaced by outward facing mirrors.

La beauté est dans la rue

The Enlightenment Project is coming to a close. It was a failed effort by some deranged people of the sun. They might have caught on to us, thought they could be like us. Alas, no.

This has been evident for some time. We were there in 1848 and bellowed along with that first rattle of death for the Enlightenment Project.

We will ease this passage, bring in that new dawn. Like philosophy is the handmaiden of religions, we assist. Angels, handmaidens, my metaphor is not mixed.

Q____, The Shadowman who initiated me, who pulled me out of the light, told me that many of us die young, don't make it. The pressure to do our job, once they have stepped out of the light, can become too much. The power, the duty, the loneliness, the knowledge that no one will ever understand; not that you could tell them anyway.

Just shadows of Shadow Men, those who left us too young, left their share in our work undone.

We were born this way. A destiny before time and outside of time. Are we special? We might be the worst of you. Destiny is a sentence. It is cold here in these shadows.

Shadow Men control the metaphor. They build it, change it, reaffirm it. The metaphor is an edifice in which we house truth, protect it from exposure, from the light.

We bring out this army of bricks and stones and build this city of metaphors, protecting truth, it moves from tower to tower, it is in all the towers, three-card monte, the shell game.

Like her, my day job wants to know what I write. In my situation at this institution, publish or perish takes on greater meaning none but my shadow brothers and sisters can ever understand. My relationships are all a cover, be they romantic or professional. Hiding amongst humanity I must live like others live. I love her. I love my job. I go out for drinks at happy hour. I appreciate positive evaluations from my students. I am in the light, but I am of shadows.

There once was an artist who hated art

There once was an artist who hated art.
This made him sad. But he was already sad.

This made him sadder.

Every day he woke up with one overwhelming
        desire to make something beautiful.
His mind instantly starts on it: *the thing of beauty.*
Then he would see a bird out the window and think
        of how pretty that bird is,
            how that bird is no different from a chicken,
            how millions of chickens are slaughtered
            every day
            but first live sad torturous lives in factory
            farms.

His work of art would make no difference to this
reality.
        the thing of beauty.
Bringing something beautiful into the world, working
on it
            all day, and the next day, and the next,
            until it is done
Is time away from saving chickens and stopping their
suffering.
His art does not feed the hungry. This he knows and
he
            reminds himself every day.
            it does not build roads,
            bandage the wounded,

clean up landmines.

Soon the world had him by the throat
And he couldn't do anything.

Unable to work, he distracted himself with
people, drinking, drugs, television.

Eventually he wasn't an artist any more.
He hated art. And this made him sad.
But he was sad already.

The Shadow Men are the handmaidens of the
forgotten. We facilitate Ubertragung. We ferry the
return of the repressed. There are many that slumber
in half-light. Brother Fanon, before he died too young,
like so many of ours, gave one last warning. He
warned the people of the sun, he warned the
perpetuators of Enlightenment of the slumbering
people of the Third World, yellow to brown to black.
At the same time he subtly warned about us. This is

our fight these days.

In our subtle machinations we weave in the unwoven.

The story is that Brother Thoreau was in jail and Brother Emerson visited him. When asked, what are you doing in there? His response was, what are you doing out there?

It is an easy answer to both questions. Brother Thoreau is in there doing our work. Brother Emerson is out there doing our work.

Contemporaneous Shadow Men have often argued about methods. We also argue across time, like family.

Brother Emerson said poets are liberating gods. Sneaky of him, huh? Poets, princes, angels, handmaidens, detectives, we all have our codes. The Ojibwa even used the term jugglers. Brother Gramsci used intellectuals. Poor Brother Gramsci, such a sad fate. We can't save our own while we try to save everyone else. He understood. It is part of the initiation.

Shadow Men see the complete present by seeing beneath the present, behind the present, around the present. We see the whole past and some of the future for this, enough for planning, enough for hope, enough for fear. Again, for planning.

Our goal is altruistic and protective, and yet we often must do battle with those we protect. At times we are like parents to impetuous children. We must force them to take their vitamins and stay out of the road.

"The world is what you will and the metaphor will hold."

She has been more and more curious about my writing. She snuggles up and asks questions, cutesy, noodling, nudging, trying to intimately draw material out.

"What is it about?"
"Is it about us?"
"Am I in it?"

Of course she is in it. She was in it before I even met her. I had observed her in this town, recorded her, made my report, performed my duty, before that night we met.

, enough for hope, enough for fear. Again, for planning.

★

Our goal is altruistic and protective, and yet we often must do battle with those we protect. At times it is like parents to impetuous children. We must force them to take their vitamins and stay out of the road.

★

"The world is what you will and the metaphor will hold."

★

She has been more and more curious about my writing. She snuggles up and asks questions, cutesy, noodling, annoying, trying to intimately draw material out. What's it about? Is it about us? Am I in it?

Of course she is in it. She was in it before I even met her. I had observed her in this town, record her, made my report, performed my duty, before that night we met.

Ah, that night, such a typical meeting for this university town, like so many typical meetings for so many American university towns. We met at a bar. The Local, and had already been in each other's closing orbits with shared friends and acquaintances.

She a grad student, me teaching in a different department. A small orbit itself. A small town, just a microcosm of that microcosm that is the City.

She liked that I taught. She liked what I taught. She liked that I wrote and who I liked to read. She is not that much younger, but as a graduate student she wants around her what she might become or who she wants to be. As a professor I can give her that.

Our attraction began physically and has continued so. It also began with the greatest sensory receptor, nerve-ending stimulator. Our brains connected, and deeply. As deeply as I can with anyone.

Our love is a thin tightrope I walk. She does not know that she spectates a highwire act. That is how sure my footing is.

Some have rumored that Brother Ducasse was a police spy, undercover. Of course he was a spy, he was one of us. Otherwise, that slander and suspicion served well in confusion as to his true nature as a Shadow Man. He suffered his true identity, suffered unto death, at twenty-four, alone in that hotel.

Sometimes I almost despair, how can we save anyone if we can't even save our own. He knew the price, we all do, and we do it for them.

"South of the north, yet north of the south, lies the CITY...peering out from the shadows of the past into the promise of the future," said Brother Du Bois.

He tried to give so much, so tirelessly, to such a hostile people of the sun. He showed them a mirror, he showed them data, and still he made barely a dent in trying to save them from themselves.

We stand by Brother Petrarch's credo: To love is to transform, to be a poet.

We can add poet to the litany of little ways to give up the ghost.

As we talk to each other through time, he was echoing Brother Ovid, who reminded that to love is also to be transformed as was that sad Brother's fate. In the hinterlands, on the distant sea, singing songs of our glory in an alien tongue now lost to time. Another punished by those we serve.

Brother Heine once described to the public—giving up the ghost—how we cross borders.

"Ye fools, so closely to search my trunk! Ye will find in it nearly nothing: My contraband goods I carry about in my head, not hid in my clothing."

We will find pen and paper, laptop, on the other side. We have all types of communication at our disposal. We smuggle with ease what is most integral.

Shadow Men are moving, traveling all the time.

Travel is a dreamscape, images, people, worlds blowing by, meaning shifting with the gazer's gaze. The world belongs to those that pay attention.

That is us.

Sometimes in my lowest moments of despair my heart races that I will be found out. The world hasn't been kind to our like. But we are our own worst enemies. Serving and suffering are interchangeable when dealing with humanity.

Back in the early part of this common era, one of us, a Brother or Sister, led a group of people from the westernmost coast of Asia, at the Mediterranean, back east.

He or she was an unintentional leader, helping liberate in a time of awful strife, so many deluded people of the sun doing so much damage. This group settled safely and secretly at some good waters in what is now Iraq. Confident that he or she was not a leader, the Shadow Wo/Man moved on. This Shadow cast a lasting impression on these people though.

It seems now the remaining Mandeans describe their god from this Brother/Sister's image when they say that he is half man, half book and sits along the waters between the two worlds reading himself.

Shadow Men build, set, transport, send, drop, ignite transcendent bombs. Those bombs burn through words, images, and minds first, tearing transcendent into the untouchable.

After they are in the mind, through all those other channels, in the mind finally, then they can go anywhere. The bomb is made flesh when it enters the mind. Once in the flesh of the mind, the bomb can resonate within a whole body, into flexed arms and clenched fists. The bomb can enter the ground, the earth itself. From the mind it is flesh, then it is hard.

The bomb can blow earth into the shape of a wall, a building, a tower, a city.

The bomb can blow a city into a building, into the shape of a wall, into nothing but earth.

The bomb blows debris out of fingertips and wide-open mouths, shrapnel that can cut through anything, embed anywhere.

Every time I hear the train I get restless. It is hard for a Shadow Man to stay in one place. It is nice to have a studio, office, workshop, but those can move with us.

We each have a beat and this is mine now and

I follow my orders. We are nothing without our assignments.

BOMB MADE FLESH

Some Shadow Men can pass in and out of the light but it is a danger. It is the most dangerous course of action for us. Most Shadow Men remain anonymous and that has been our best and safest bet since the beginning.

Those who pass in and out of the light run the greatest risks. They let their names be known and at least their surface contributions be obvious. This makes the double life and the work harder. Hardest for those who step out of the light and embrace the shadow early, at a young age.

    Poor Brother Ducasse, poor Brother Holderlin.

She says she loves me. I say it back. I don't know how it is possible for her really, to love someone you don't know even half of. How could you love someone who keeps so many secrets? Everything I write. Everything that moves in my head. Every assignment. This life is hard for sharing. She is easy or maybe so clever she has one-upped one such as I, but I doubt it. I envy her her honesty, her truth, and authenticity of existence. Not I.

    I am a Shadow Man.

She has been asking about my book.

One thing that she seems to actually know about me is that I have a destiny. It makes her feel special to share me with a destiny, a call toward some greatness, even if she has no hope of understanding it.

But she does hope to understand it. She asks about my book. She wants it to be, to come to life, into existence. I will produce it for her, and for my destiny. She will learn of me through it, no matter how fantastic the tale. The art of the Shadow Men reveals as much as it conceals. It is part of our way, our assistance, the duty. She will have some reveals just for her, my wit, my erudition, my prose conjuring pathos and glimpses of humanity in the raw out of mere words on the page.

And there will be conceals just for her and most readers of the plight and the workings of the Shadow Men. Hidden reveals to other Shadow Men, little tears in the curtain just for them, little apocalypses in the oldest, truest definition of that word as we have used it for over two thousand years.

Shadow Men are eyes that can see in the darkness. We see best in the darkness, actually.

Cosmic   Shudder

Naked Terror

The worst of the people of the sun want to convince you that Everything is True (and therefore nothing is permitted).

Our job is to disseminate the Truth that Nothing is True (and therefore everything is permitted).

In actuality, we know that there is no middle, but some things are true and some things are Not permitted.

Why else would we bother? Why else would we have bothered for thousands of years?

The saddest irony of the people of the sun is that they cannot see. The Shadow Men see in all directions at all times. The people of the sun think they are alone, to a horrific degree and to horrific ends. Shadow Men think of all humans everywhere at all times. It is a crushing unthinkable weight.

This is why so many of our ranks implode, especially those who step out of the light too early, too young.

Secrets are like bombs, their ontology is their teleology. When they come into their own true being, when they actualize, they cease to be.

I have been keeping the Shadow Man secret well for so long, but she makes it different. Shadow Men are alone in the world, but sometimes we must pretend that we are not by sharing our lives. This I do with her. I share my life but I have created a secret. She doesn't know there is a secret so it doesn't really exist. Secret or no, I feel safe with her.

But the thinking of secrets and bombs, their similar ironic and unstable definitions/identities, has led me onto a path to keep my secret better. A prose piece I began several years ago called *BOMB*. I know her curiosity has been running away with her. Reading the unspoken imaginations of other people is one of the great talents of the Shadow Men. I need to produce for her, for a public too, to maybe even walk in the light (put my name in the light), do the more public aspects of our work. Until then I must produce for her, calm her imagination that what I write is fiction instead of this Shadow work.

So my mind goes back to some prose I made before I stepped out of the light, *BOMB*. What I have in my records is the title, *BOMB*, the subtitle, *The End of the Infinite*, then a Prologue followed by a poem also titled, "Bomb."

BOMB
The end of the infinite

    There was a time when all I knew was Bomb. That time has yet to end.

    I have many, many parts inside me, components of a whole, a vast structure. All the many, many parts have individual roles and a distinct ennobled anima, building in essence the effect of strong whole individuals making a stronger individual whole. The mind of each part is infinite and runs the dangerous gamut of all possibilities possible for directed concentration. Scrolling, scrolling the ever-reaching number-line of possible possibilities; this process happens instantly for each of the many, many, almost infinite amount of parts. Every second each part has begun and completed this world-reaching action at least twice. Like the synaptic firings in a brain or a world tilting on its axis, ever so fast and gentle, the individual processes of the individual parts seem to begin and end within the same instance. The journeys into infinity begin with the aim for a point of which to designate concentration and energy. In each rapid process rapidly occurring in each of the many, many parts the point is sought and achieved each time by each of the many, many parts. The designated point of concentration arrived at by each individual part for each individual process is always the same. All the different minds, the infinite minds, that make up the finite whole, all consistently, continuously, and gratuitously share the same thought. That thought is Bomb.

Bomb

In the beginning there was Bomb
After Bomb there was nothing
Maybe I should start at the beginning

In the beginning there was Bomb

Our mouths tasted of copper
We dripped the juice that once bound
Every direction marked our passing
We burst forth, hot and ready

Spinning and ripping, carving nothing
Alone but strong, with hubris and momentum
We beat on as if there could be no end
Charging the mystery of limits

But our history was our home
Tethered to what we once were
We snapped back upon ourselves
Snapped back into nothing

In the beginning there was Bomb
After Bomb there was nothing
Maybe I should start at the end
In the beginning there was Bomb

"What was scattered gathers, what was gathered
blows apart."
Heraklitus

BOMB was to be a big novel. A novel you shouldn't read on a plane, and certainly not out loud. A novel for furtive glances and whispers and head-nods in your direction. Maybe it would need a paper bag cut and folded into a book cover like for textbooks in elementary school. Or when published, the airport bookstore edition would have just a solid black cover with raised lettering spelling the title, BOMB, but only to the touch, not visually discernible. Not that the dream of BOMB would have been a commercial book. Certainly not a thriller. I was following in the footsteps of William S. Burroughs, who I had yet to know was a fellow brother, but the kinship was there since the first time I read him. He made me understand that many components can be brought together as in collage, pastiche, or montage from other mediums in a literary setting where they link by theme or the occasional adjoined character to explore a particular point. Like scanning a crowd in a particular location, a narrative, novelistic setting is one of intersections and grouping.

BOMB, to me, was everything, and contained

the scope of the universe and our momentary appearance in its trajectory from solid un-being-all-mass origins until it reaches its border of space or bounds of velocity and snaps back into itself. A pendulum, an eternal return. Going out and going back in: there we are watching ourselves in a double-mirror with one side hope and the other despair.

So in this novel I would have to include the cold stone beginning. And the stone cold end. And of course a historical fiction telling of Robert J. Oppenheimer's life and study of the Bhagavad Gita and moment of intimate encounter with BOMB, a micro reenactment of the universe's origin and destruction, matter turned inside out. Like the narrator of the Mahabharata, Vyasa, Oppenheimer stands in the middle of the story, our story, BOMB's story, and he knows the ending, he can tell it. He is a prophet and a pawn, a speck of dust and just as much a god. Vyasa was a Shadow Man.

There were several other set pieces drafted to fill out the novel, *BOMB*. One of my favorites was called "Righteous Burst." The story was titled for the street name of a party drug existing not only in the novel, but also in the deep dreams of drug addicts, chemists, religious leaders, the CIA, video-gamers, nihilists, anarchists, artists. The drug, "Righteous Burst," when consumed by tablet—a tablet that can also be crushed up and snorted, free-based, mainlined, inserted into the vagina or anus as a suppository, wiped on the gums, baked into pastries or your morning oatmeal—breaks down systems in the human brain. It is the ultimate escape, relaxation, or high. Over the duration of its activation, Righteous Burst allows the user to feel no commitments, obligations, associations, connections, or relations. All systematic thinking and relevant action is destroyed. It is utter freedom, waking death.

It is presented as the total nightmare of anti-drug propagandists, an unstoppable Yes/No/Fuck You in one pill, yet it delivered to the user a bliss of such simple, total, primal, chaotic freedom that its appeal is hard to deny after any first-person testimonials. For spectators and users alike (after coming down and surveying ones memory), the actions committed during a Righteous Burst high are horrific. During the high there is no possible conception of a right or a wrong, no up or a down, no possible or impossible and everything, EVERYTHING, feels so fucking good. Sisters fuck brothers, animals are eaten alive, fires are started and blaze as a gorgeous spectacle consuming whatever is in their path, and the less meaning anything has, the better it feels.

I don't know if I am ever going to finish *BOMB*. I don't know if I can. And so what if I did? It couldn't sell, that much I know. Who would read such a thing? I would have to be much more established first before inflicting that on an audience. I would need something else first, something easier, something fun.

Brother Ivan Illich endeavored to write an epilogue of the industrial age.

This is one of the main tasks of the Shadow Men today. We endeavor at once to bring in the post-Enlightenment Age/Era/Period and to prepare all the people of the sun to transition seamlessly into it without even noticing. We have been partly there for some time, transitions are slow, that is the only way. The Earth moves and most can't even feel it. The Axis is tilting. One day we will be upside down and no one will ever remember being right-side up.

Sister Carrington worked to remind us that humans are still just beasts, and even if they reach their worst potential there will always be Shadows to shade from the most burning and blinding light. When the axis tilts, and life upends, we will still be there to lead across the new tundras. We will show the way to community and daily magic. We will help carve home in any rock or glacier and we will retreat back into the shadows; loving from a distance; loving from within.

Brother Gramsci described us well: We display the pessimism of thought yet work with the optimism of will. That has always been our strategy.

Shadow Men know the whole world is readable. That expression, an old, moldy chestnut: I can read you like a book. Well, that is how the world is for us. Every detail, movement, bumper sticker, clothing choice, facial expression, complex semiotic, is all text to us. That is how we know the future. It is like guessing the next line in a song. The future is an inevitable next piece in the sequence of world text we read. Magic is praxis.

Nox involvit umbra diem

Our work is one great Shadow Book. It is thousands of years long. Our great work is half unwritten, it is lived words of deed. This is just selections from my chapter.

One of the difficult parts of our work is to express universal and ancient truths in the language of this time to the people of this time.

The last girlfriend I had before I stepped out of the light was a pathological liar.

    I learned a lot from her. She was not one of our own. She was sketchy, not shadowy. Her lies served no end, no true end. I learned by tracking her, learned from her mistakes, and learned about myself. My latent, yet already near the surface, Shadow Man instincts were worked. I wrote about her, recorded her, and also turned what I learned from report into prose.

This love that knew nothing but lies inspired in me and from me a half-work destined never to be finished. As I sought to understand her and the nature of duplicity I developed a character who had committed his whole career to such a study. This character came to love and embrace the idea of the lie, it became who he was. After she would fall asleep I would stay up late and pour all of my confusion into this character's own lectures and through it all I found an understanding. This character was referred to as Dr. Lies and I removed myself once more by telling about him through his own assistant.

The Great Dr. Lies

Betrayal is part of life, he said, but he didn't stop there. The Buddha said all life is an illusion and it was one of his rare moments of didactic kindness—all about compassion that guy, but not when he lectured, hardnosed he was—but it was kindness. Life is not an illusion, it is a lie. Truth is elusive, ever-elusive, greased and slippery, greased and slippery, like one of those filthy, tarty Jell-O or baby oil wrestlers. Whores, all whores. These were the moments when he spoke and it was painfully obvious for all that he was syphilitic. He could not keep that bile down. *Life is a lie,* he proceeded, *a finite, though seemingly infinite series of lies, one after another. Each act is an act of concealment, as I said, Truth is elusive. The paranoids are right, but please don't tell them that, please, they have enough to worry about and of course they'd be right, they are. People like to wax all mature, especially when they talk about interpersonal relationships—after a fight with their parents or husband or wife—and say that line we all know, that you can't know everything about another person. And ya know, ya can't know everything about anything.* He said that part in his best Midwestern accent to try to sound as common as he could, as if he actually could. *So let's say they are right,* he went on, *people love to cite "they," and they are right, ya know, ya can't know everything about anything, there's got to be some mystery in the world.* He relished the word mystery in his best Midwestern relish and joy as if for the common folk the word itself was as mysterious as the phenomenon it was to signify. *So let's take these commoners, the heartland folk, volk, and their reliable source "they" as correct, why shouldn't we, there are more of them than us— and begin from there before returning to Buddha and Truth.*

We can never know everything about anything— and in that regard—any body, any person. But the world is finite, humans, people are finite, there is only so much involved with any one body. But people, life, things are a mysterious well of information, finite but seemingly infinite.

Still with me? he asked, but not actually caring, the expression for him was more of a devise for pacing.

These finite things, all things for that matter, allude—I return to that word out of kindness for the subject—to the infinite. In all honesty and respect for things, a category in which I include people, they are therefore deceptive. They are finite, their components and characteristics are quantifiable and therefore totally knowable and their initial deception is their appearance as infinite. Back to life before the density of my tapeworm of rambled words threatens to devour us all. Life is a lie, every morsel of knowledge we have about anything—and remember, anything is potentially knowable in toto—conceals in omission as much as it reveals. The smallest crumb of data only confirms what we don't know, which is everything else. Every fact is a lie of omission. If ya can't know everything about someone then anything they tell you is a tease, misinformation, a bluff, an appetite-whetting smoke screen. We could trust, defer to optimism. Maybe they are telling the whole story, if there was more to tell why wouldn't they? Maybe I see a house with people home, the lights are on. Why would the lights be on if no one is home? At face value I can believe optimistically in the goodness of our fellow man and believe that no one would leave the lights of their home on while they were out so from a distance on faith in goodness, a well-lit house is not empty. Why should I suppose there is more to the story, why not trust? I am sorry Trust, Our Fellow Man, Humanity, but face value is a lie. There is always more to any story, another dimension, density to be fleshed out. Our parents taught us—in all their god-like worldliness—that omissions are lies, we can lie by omission. No one will deny the art of conversation, rhetoric, literature; the craftiness, the cunning of speech, language; twisted words, backhanded compliments, it always conceals as much as it reveals. So language is a lie. Even if it gives a little, it takes away our trust, or faith in expression, in communication, in the fact that there is anything real or true outside of ourselves and it is a good thing that it does this because in concealing it *actually reveals a greater truth, that there is nothing real or true outside of ourselves.*

Ya can't ever really know anyone. And why not? They, like everything else, are finite, knowable. Because they lie, everything hides and deceives. Nothing is what it seems; because it doesn't want to be, it cannot. You might broach the question of time, maybe even though things are finite they are still proceeding in time and therefore since we are also trapped in time we don't literally have the time to learn everything about something. Of course, some of you might want to veer into hypotheticals. If I could take something out of time or stand out of time myself I could then record the complete data on my subject, a Maxwell's Demon of data-analysis. It's a fun game, but nevertheless, hypotheticals are just a fun game. I cannot remove myself or my subject from time but from my vantage point within time it is quite apparent that time is part of the great lie. What was it that time-obsessed German-hoot-owl Hegel once said, "Time is the negative element in a sensuous world"? Damned if he wasn't right. As we lurch forward, it detracts, opening up a whole new universe of finite choices from each choice that leads us to the next moment. A different world each moment, each one dying just a little bit more and fighting that taunting moribund rattle with each new universe's new set of choices draped as another thick veil. There is no apocalypse, no revelation. Each moment is another layer, each layer a whole new set of diversions—

Lies, he punctuates his speech with loudly—*and we do not have the time to peel them back as they continue to stack up.*

Of course the layers are finite, but so are we. He stopped here and coughed. He sipped from the water at his podium but this was his own deception. He had the brunt of his point and ended it with a note of possible humor. The cough, the water, all ruse. Even if his throat was dry it was no bother to him. His true discomfort was in his pants. Only I there knew his strength in resisting the fidget, the scratch, the shuffle. He is a man who is never comfortable, probably never has been and somehow found greater and greater ways to reduce the original minimal comfort all the while denying his care for comforts. He is not that strong though. Deny all he wants, the pains have taken their toll on him. All he is is mind, the old man, his few supporters backhandedly applaud. I am sure that minority would admit that even his mind is corrupt and decaying as well as the form that jarringly propels it. His audience now is one drawn to spectacle. The lurching spouting bile of a once great name, and name I mean, it still draws more than the man ever could. He would say reputation is a lie. As you would imagine he quite often ends any kind of conversation or discussion in the same way. For a while it is profound, then funny in its lingering profundity, and soon enough trying on one's patience before it eventually becomes childlike with a feeling of empty redundancy. You might wonder if it was the same with the bile—or spleen, as he is so fond of saying the French are fond of saying—that he spews for some one as close to him as myself, this progression from profundity to a juvenile annoyance, but due to the depth of my intimacy, as least as far as habitation is concerned, it is frighteningly different. The bile is not an act, it is him at his tamest, his kindest, his rarest moment of compassion for blind sniveling humanity in all its gruff self-inflated stupidity, to use his words I hear so often. Beneath the bile, the almost grouchy artifice created for the bile, is true seething hate. We could say psychologically that the hate is for himself and he is so solipsistic that he believes there is nothing but the self so which ever way he directs that hate it is still coming back to the source. Psychologically, that is an easy tactic, but as a witness, as an inside source, I have a different view. It is hate pure and simple. It would be nice to say that was what was keeping him alive but that wouldn't be accurate, it is not keeping him alive. His hate is killing him. He is slowly dying. He would say we all are, but with him it is a visible process. I watch him die. There is nothing I can do about it. He has made his choice, many of them, and most did not praise life, let alone stand in any way toward delaying all of our inevitable fates. His hate is the deepest part of him from what I can tell and I respect his efforts to hide it from the world, even me. He doesn't know that I can always hear him, it is part of my job. And every night it is the same, every night. If he remembers his dreams he must know what is inside himself, that it has never been a secret to himself, and he must then lie to me every morning when I ask if he slept alright, any eventful dreams, or some other such question along those lines. Every morning he says he slept fine, no dreams he can remember worth mentioning. Either he lies to lend greater mystery to himself on my behalf, or he lies not realizing I can hear him or he actually remembers nothing. Whatever the case may be in the morning, it does not change what I hear at night, actually the calm of the morning magnifies the darkness of the night.

At night as he sleeps, he talks, not just speech, words, but grunts, growls, hisses, and other such gutturals to punctuate his midnight nocturnes. I am being kind for the sake of eloquence. Dirge would be the closest musical metaphor or something more contemporaneous like death metal. Sans eloquence, in all bare truth he speaks what I can only describe as hate. A pure, radiant hate so real to him I can feel it through the walls and it fills me with nausea. Tea, chamomile, warm milk, and a pharmacornucopia have been employed by me over the years to coerce sweet sleep to capture me amid the raining filthy torrent and its affects upon my stomach lining. All I can imagine is that the world has failed him, one person at a time and he truly believes everything is a lie, not an illusion (so passive) but a lie (very intentional) and therefore he trusts nothing and has no where to stand, he is falling through a dissolving world, not empty, but hostile. As he sleeps he hates. His body rests and his mind uses his mouth and vocal chords and otherwise resting lungs to belch forth hate, the depth of his being. Nothing is safe from his hate, as soon as REM sleep happens it is released and it ends just before his alarm every morning. Anything that anyone could perceive to be sacred is violated in his speech. I can barely draw specifics, it is odd since I hear them every night, but the words hate in such a reaching unfocused way that I gnash my teeth to keep them out of my head and only succeed to the details, the sense of them is always there and sinks down to my guts like a drowning baby tied to a stone. The hate is so strong I can justifiably describe the sense of it that he does not believe that love exists and the worst part of all is that he once did believe in its existence and to no longer believe is a true loss. Maybe he can think now he never believed, that he lied to himself, didn't really believe, and if he could convince himself of such a grand lie then anything could be fabricated and there is no where to put one's trust.

Why not ennui then? Why hate? Does he still love, does he wrestle with it? Are all his pains ever fresh, no matter how concealed by day the night lays them bare to be felt over and over again? Does he continuously hear every lie again, believe it, learn it is untrue, and fall a little farther all night long? Maybe it is hero-worship on my part to believe hate is fight. I don't know, maybe hate is love?

By piecing together fragments from many nights I have understood a little about his personality, the pathos of his deep hate and its connection to love. The word ghost has reoccurred. A ghost beside him. He has many times spouted hate at the non-entity sleeping next to his lone frame. He can feel them, or her I should deduce, but to reach out and try to touch his hand goes right through her.

Another lecture by the doctor:

Duplicity is an understatement, man is multifarious. Every man, with all the pulls, is a traitor to his heart, his mind, his past, his future, his family, his heritage, and his self in every action. We can never know who we are talking to or even who we are. Heraclitus was just the tip of the iceberg. Every man has one nature and that is no nature. Once we accept this we can do everything, or at least anything. Chaos theory, atomic theory, the Pre-Socratics, Buddhism, the Upanishads, and contemporary physicists, are all showing more of the iceberg. We are barely here. If you want truth it is in the moment. Only the moment is true, nothing else, and this truth is gone as soon as it is here. Everything, nothing all at once. All reality, all time, all happenings, coming and going. I am not Dr. Lies as they call me. What I say right now is true, people only speak the truth. Entirely true in the saying because at the moment it is the only thing that is real. So gone, so unreal, so untrue in a second. Leaving everyone rats, snitches, canaries, song birds, and rubes, marks, and overlords, handlers, managers, all at the same time. Mysteries, spy movies, cop shows with narcs—these obsess us, our culture, our world, they always have, from Sophocles to King Lear to television and paperback novels and it is because all of these dramas go on at the same time in each and every one of us. Jung with his archetypes. Yes, they are all inside us and they are true and they battle and they all win and lose all the time and we are as little our selves as this day is Tuesday. We give names but we wouldn't know and today doesn't know. Yesterday didn't. It is too warm to be a day in October. Well maybe the day has its season but it probably doesn't know what we expect of it, nor does it care. Christianity, that ridiculous faith of building big churches on sweet-spun ideas based all of its great new theology on one simple act resulting from a betrayal. Those Christ-lovers should thank Judas every day, praying to him only in his actions of betrayal for their salvation. Jesus couldn't have done it without him. Jesus' job was easy, he was arrested and killed. Didn't fight back, didn't lift a hand except to carry his own cross, but Judas, he had the labor, he had to work both sides, middleman the deal for salvation. Give up his friend, show himself for the traitor that we all are. And he was marked for that, like Cain, marked as a true honest human. Honest as his multilayered self. Jesus knew it and chose Judas for his humanity. If anything, Jesus played Judas. It is a simple equation to put responsibility on Judas. Does a lamb provide dinner or does the butcher? We eat the lamb but he is the fruits of the butcher's labor.

He once tried to write a children's story. He beat his head against the wall for some weeks and many, many balls of paper wound up in this trash basket before he seemed happy (happy for him) or had finally just stopped. It is hard to tell whether he was actually satisfied with what he wrote, actually liked it, actually meant to say just that, or failed to even conceive of what lesson he had for a child. I have included here the complete transcript.

Children's Story by the Doctor:

There is a land opposite ours where everyone speaks honest and true all the time. The people there go about naked because they have nothing to hide.
They also have no faces.

The Doctor was also fond of making lists.
Here are a few of his lists:

Lies Impossible to Contest:
--I love you
--I hate you
--I believe in God
(all opinions and beliefs)

Lies Dangerous to Challenge:
--I am allergic to that
--I am scared of heights
--I am agoraphobic
(all conditions and diseases)

Lies Difficult to Contest:
--I was napping alone
--I am a virgin
--I am not a virgin

Since language was the greatest lie as far as the Doctor was concerned he even dabbled in ways to streamline it, even the alphabet.

"The Doctor's Aim to Improving the English Language Through Alphabet Modification"

The doctor had been concerned as of late with purifying the English language. By English language he is not referring to the spoken language, but about the alphabet in particular, and how it corresponds to the spoken language. He finds the English alphabet to be too bulky and redundant, existing in some places only to serve antiquated rules, yet sadly, no longer the speaker. His aim and passion is to streamline the alphabet for greater efficiency. This will benefit any new learner or experienced speaker the same. The changes he proposes will be phonetic and visually easy for any reader or pronouncer. Be aware that the doctor is not a linguist. He employs language and basic linguistics in his work, as do all academics, but linguistics is no specialty of his.

From the start his first concern is getting rid of the Q. It is a letter originally from French influence and not only redundant in its phonic employ, but also codependent in every usage. The Q cannot be used without a U. The U can be used on its own. This makes the Q the weaker party in the relationship. It is not only weaker but also expendable. He finds the expendable nature of the Q to be akin to waste. His pursuit in this matter of simplifying seems very utilitarian. "Quiet" could just as easily be spelled as "kwiet." In this other spelling the K and the W signify the same sound together as do the Q and U, and though they make a sound together that depends on two letters, they are two letters that can be used on their own on other occasions. *If we are to lie*, says the Doctor, *as we do in all utterances and writings, at least let's keep it tidy.*

I never finished any of this work on the great doctor of lies and I have no intention of continuing such work. That girlfriend eventually left me and soon after I stepped out of the light. Becoming a Shadow Man, I saw all of the truth in lies and solidified all of these ideas simmering within me that had escaped through these strange filters as prose. One day I might pillage the Doctor Lies material for select sentences and illustrative concepts as needed.

Soon after that breakup I wrote this poem:

Another Truth

Another truth
Another truth
Always another truth
Around every corner
Under every stone
Faint in each touch
Loud in each gasp
Another truth
Another truth

To live in a world

without lies
On her lips another truth
Another truth in her eyes

Nothing is true everything is permitted
No, everything is true and nothing is permitted
To see you, to know it's true
There are no lies, in your eyes

In every book,
        in every day
In every look,
        in every way
Another truth
Another truth
"I am truer than you"
        but your shout falls at her feet.

She looks that way and it is true
She speaks this way and it is true
She looks at me and touches you
It is true, it is true, so much, yes, true

Another truth

Je est un autre
And an other is you

True, true

There was a Shadow Wo/Man in Tahrir Square and for months a Shadow Wo/Man slept in Zuccotti Park. Our time is always, and it is very much now.

We are always contemporaneous. We wave back from just over the horizon.

There is no difference between reading the present and reading the past or future. That is part of our training.

One of the hardest parts of stepping out of the light is that a life in the Shadows can court true darkness. It has brought many of us down early. For as long as we can we wrestle with it. Brother Nietzsche called it the Abyss, Brother Benjamin called it the Destructive Character, and even Brother Poe called it the Imp of the Perverse.

and thought work well for us. As we move the world, and help the world move itself in the right direction we gravitate always to the newest fulcrums.

★

There was a Shadow Man in Tahrir Square and for months a shadow man slept in Zuccotti Park. Our time is always and it is very much now.

We are always contemporaneous. We wave back from just over the horizon.

★

There is no difference between reading the present and reading the past or future. That is part of our training.

★

One of the hardest parts of stepping out of the light is that a life in the shadows can court true darkness. It has brought many of us down early, for as long as we can we wrestle with it. Brother Nietzsche called it the Abyss, Brother Benjamin called it the Destructive Character and even Brother Poe called it the Imp of the Perverse.

It has had many more names.

Sweet Sister Sylvia suffered so sorrowfully and sovereignly. I didn't know she was a Shade when I first read the *Bell Jar* at seventeen; but I didn't know I was one yet either. She did try to tell me though: "I thought the most beautiful thing in the world must be shadow."

Reading a book is no different from reading a painting or a symphony or a person or a situation or a city.

At the Library:

The grey wave of dying buildings in the wind.
The buildings are worked in, but there no one lives.
Dead words, thoughts stilled on paper,
Edifices of text, numbers dimly glowing.

We speak much recently of the tragedy of Brother Debord. It is never easy to work in the light, that is why most of us seek no fame, no name, and move in forever shadows. Shadow life, our duty is perilous in itself, living amongst people of the sun, ever uncomfortable and taxing. For those that choose to lead, who take on the more public of our duties, alcoholism, escapist addiction, are the quickest pitfalls, madness being a frequent possibility, especially for those who step out of the light too young.

Brother Debord tried to have many things

both ways, tried too hard to walk shaded in the light or push too readily too much out of the light. His end was not uncommon for Shadow Men. Failure is part of our work. His end was an end, sadly, often for the most acclaimed of our ranks.

One of the techniques we have employed that Brother Debord brought into the light in his own way is "drift." His "technique of a transient passage through varied ambiances," worked well for '50s and '60s Paris, mimicking one of our major components since the dawn of time.

"Everything, but really everything is on the move. There is nothing outside of time." Hans Haacke never heard of us.

"J'ai vu l'ombre d'un cocher, qui avec, l'ombre d'une brosse frottait l'ombre d'une carrosse."

We must always remember the fate of Brother Bruno. It is so very possible for any of us that choose to walk in the light, to publish books to help the people of the sun. He tried so hard. Even before his fiery fate he was nicknamed "the exasperated," a feeling common to us all as we do our work and engage humanity. Like many of us, he felt, "In tristitia hilaris, in hilaritate tristis."

In my work, like many others before me, I have practiced and studied his techniques in *On the Shadow of Ideas*.

We bring joys, we give deep and haunting cheer to the world. As Meander once let on, having encountered one of our own, you can be happy to just encounter the shadow of a friend.

We ebb and flow, our power, and in relation to others:
In solis sis tibi turba locis

We are now living together. She and I.
I am never alone and forever lonely. She never tires of my shadow.

The effort of artists, the work of Shadow Men, IS the sound of a tree falling in the forest with no one around to hear it.

Oh, we feedest on, Night after Night, our only book: The light of supreme darkness.

To live in the light, among people of the sun, regularity is necessary, normalcy. It is necessary for the dual life. We understand people by their patterns and we live amongst them by creating our own patterns, fitting our patterns among and in between theirs. Normalcy is what so many aspire for that in living the double life it becomes the perfect disguise. Be honest. Be honest all the time. Be known for being honest and then no one will expect the lie, or the deception. They will see only the truth, because that is normal. That is the pattern you have established. No one will suspect the work we do. No one will question where we go, where we've been.

As we commit to lives in the light we look orderly and we give honest taste, as those of us who have stepped into the light have done in publishing our work. We hide our true work in fiction, poetry, essay, critique, philosophy, all the fun narrative manipulations, that spoonful of sugar under which we hide the medicine of truth.

Sister Myles reminds me that "the secret of the modern world is that we are all alone." We Shadow Wo/Men are always alone and suffer with the people of the sun.

Always *com passio*

The silence of Joan, her resistance in inquisition, her inability to describe the voice, these are marks of her Shadow identity. Some pass into the light to act in the world, act beyond the calling, sometimes denying the calling.

Violence is in the light. Inaction is the darkness. Our work in the shadows transcends both.

The shadow is a darkness that owns the light.

Sometimes in my darkest moments I go to speak with Joan. Through the flames I hear her screams and they are perfectly clear. She tells me not to be afraid. Our work matters. I'm not alone. These people she sought to serve, they know not what they do.

All forms, mediums, signs are ours. When Semiotics developed as a discipline we all smiled at each other back and forth across time.

Brother Artaud gave up the ghost a bit when he spoke of form, saying, "If there is still one hellish, truly accursed thing in our time, it is our artistic dallying with forms, instead of being like the victims burned at the stake, signaling through the flames."

We meet in/on a bardo as needed by the needy.

When Bowie gave up the ghost he mentioned in Quicksand, "You can tell me all about it on the next bardo."

Within the language of the physics of the people of the sun, there is no way to explain (or easy way) where we meet. That Shadows among the Buddhists use the term, "bardo." When there, are you in? On? I don't even want to get started on *when* you are?

Sometimes it feels like being engulfed in a still, cool flame.

In the 3rd century, Euhemerus figured out something about us, that many of the ancient gods were based on real people. Some of those gods are us, some are stories created by us.

"According to Dionysius, the Divine Darkness appears dark only because it is so dazzlingly bright—a paradox I have attempted to understand by looking directly at the sun and noticing the dark spot that flowers at its center." Maggie Nelson gives a slight tease-out of her shadow identity, a slight giving up of the ghost, while tracking those that have tracked us over the years.

I am the dark spot flowering at the center of the sun.

Shadow Men and Women see in dazzling darkness. When we step out of the light our eyes adjust to this dazzling darkness. It is where we work, where we live. It is lit by a radiant black star.

When we walk in the light and do our work as double agents, in this most treacherous way, we must speak, and speak loudly, but to the people of the sun our true language is unhearable, it is the language of silence.

Hermana Pizarnik:
El lenguaje silencioso engendra fuego. El silencio se propaga, el silencio es fuego.

Era preciso decir acerca del agua o simplemente apenas nombrarla, de modo de atraerse la palabra agua para que apague las llamas de silencio.

Porque no cantó, su sombra canta. Donde una vez sus ojos hechizaron me infancia, el silencio al rojo rueda como un sol.

A memory from my childhood that was a clear indicator of my path:
My father loved the movie *Three Days of the Condor* and

we watched it a lot. Redford was so cool in it, the denim jacket under the peacoat, the great '70s shag of hair. But mostly his job, what he did. He was a reader for the CIA. An actual job, a Reader. He calls it that, explains it like that. They read everything and look for systems in newspapers, novels, comic books, from all over the world. And of course his department stumbles on something, they are all killed but him, his code name is Condor and now he is out there on the streets acting like an operative to survive. His knowledge is vast and he prevails, out there reading the world, reading people.

Readers, spies, it was so enthralling. I think my father loved those things together in it. He liked other spy movies but I think he revered something about it that seemed more real, attainable. He was an academic, so that means he read for a living, but only in a very small corner of knowledge. If only he knew the distinct breed of Reader into which his son was born.

Brother Heraclitus reminds us that "people dull their wits with gibberish, and cannot use their ears and eyes." That is for us to do. Maybe living in the light is too blinding or distracting.

The eye, the ear, the mind in action; these I value.

Je est un autre.

Brother Nietzsche points out the blindness of people wandering the world; they love ignorance and do not want to perish of impatience and premature tasting of things promised. They tell this to their shadows. We listen and provide knowledge and the future with kind gradualness.

"Playing chess against oneself is as paradoxical as jumping over one's shadow."
(Stefan Zweig)

"I have learned the trick of watching shadows, and standing motionless in such a position that they cut and dapple my outline."
(Geoffrey Household)

"The Geometric Mouse is its own shadow."
(Claes Oldenburg)

"Here, the shadow does a stranger to the body it
perfects."
(Jean Cocteau)

If we shadows have offended,
Think but this and all is mended:

That you have but slumbered here
While these visions did appear.
And this weak and idle theme,
No more yielding, but a dream...

"I am the dust in the sunlight, I am the ball of the sun,
To the dust I say: Remain. And to the sun, roll on."
(Jelaleddin)

Brother Poe reminds us how difficult our work is that
some books, like dark human hearts—er lasst sich
nicht lesen—do not allow themselves to be read.

Living as part of the apparatus of the state, the truest expression of the light, brings the schizophrenia, the anxiety, the paranoia, since one is never alone, always watched, subjected, a subject, and freedom, originality, individuality, and the true art of living is sacrificed for order, safety, cold comfort, those warmest of cold comforts, that you never possess but borrow, lease from the state, like property tax on "owned" land, thus is the body, and the mind shut up in it, at home only in deviation, "real" only in crime, natural only in taboo, honest only when telling the most gorgeous of lies.

Writing on the flesh, in flesh, scars that transcend ink: "One Man in Chains, Every Man in Chains!"
There is no Word but Flesh, the logos is bled.

Alice Walker, a Shadow for her time and place, a Shadow for her people's struggle, and therefore all people's struggle, gave up the ghost of her purpose, our purpose once in an essay thusly: "The artist then is the voice of the people, but she is also The People."

I have lied to everyone I have ever loved. I have lied to everyone I have ever met.

If one were to reverse those two sentences and combine them into one compound sentence they would form a logical and transitive argument.

In German love and lie are only one letter off: liebe/liege.

Every Shadow Man is a Double Agent. Every operation is a False Flag.
    Sometimes I just want to break down and cry.

Brother Nietzsche sums us up well. He points out as advice: "Thou shalt build living memorials to thyself. But before that, thou must build up thine own body and soul."

This is the work we do for everyone. This is our work.

Everything I say I say in two ways. Every sentence, or even mere gasp is true to one and very much it is its opposite to another. To this other, every thought or action has a sister who looks in the opposite direction. Frantically, I use my divided mind, the only way to live in this world, to cover both of their backs.

Can one ever go on like this? Can one be free, whole?

A
radiant

black star.

The place of eternal light is the ultimate horror. The lights are never turned off in the basement of the secret police headquarters. Round the clock they torture, reprogram, find your greatest fears, and exploit them. It is there you renounce everything you love and care about, all that makes you who you are.

We work forever in the shadows against this eternal light. We toil half-lit, writing, composing from our vast reach into the darkness. We fight this light and always will. The people of the sun need shadowy leadership, they cannot see truth directly.

Frantically, I use my divided mind, the only way to live in this world, to cover both at their backs.

Can one ever go on like this? Can one be free, whole?

★

A radiant black star.

★

The place of eternal light is the ultimate horror. The lights are never turned off in the basement of the secret police headquarters. Round the clock they torture, reprogram, find your greatest fear and exploit them. It is there you renounce everything you love and care about, all that makes you who you are.

We work forever in the shadows against this eternal light. We toil half-lit, writing, composing from our vast reach into the darkness. We fight this light and always will. The people of the sun need shadowy leadership, they cannot see truth directly. The evil of—

The evil of them created that eternal light underground. Its symbolism is the opposite of ours. With the first grunted utterance of hate we countered with a feint, a detour, the first metaphor and thus the beginning of all literature and art. With that first metaphor we said something that was not true (but beautiful) to get at a higher truth. Parry and feint, fall back and flack, we attack unexpectedly.

Brother Nietzsche said he didn't believe in a god who didn't dance. What he really meant was that he didn't believe in anything that didn't dance.

I do not believe in a Revolution that does not dance.

"Out of the shadow of the abstract man, who thinks for the pleasure of thinking, emerges the organic man, who thinks because of a vital imbalance, and who is beyond science and art." –Brother Cioran

We live—have always lived—by exile, silence, and cunning. Always. When we move within a crowd. When we speak. When we do anything.

Exile, silence, cunning.

Kurt Vonnegut's third novel was his first with a moral. *Mother Night* turned out to have three morals actually. They are all very good and important, as is the book itself.

The first moral is: "We are what we pretend to be, so we must be careful about what we pretend to be."

The other two follow: "When you're dead you're dead."

And: "Make love when you can, it's good for you."

That book also teaches us that "espionage offers each spy an opportunity to go crazy in a way he finds irresistible."

"A dream is a playwright clothed in beautiful shadows in a theater fashioned on the wind."

POR NADIE, NUNCA.

We are alone, that is how we work. In a crowd of thousands. In a bed of two, we are always alone. We listen, watch, smell, taste, record it all from each our own moving stone citadel.

Alone.

"He who wishes to know the truth about life in its immediacy must scrutinize its estranged form." (T.W. Adorno)

My work is important.

My work is necessary.

When the demons come I must fight them, that creeping malaise or Imp of the Perverse. The abyss looking out from me. I turn to porn, drugs, escape in all its worst forms: domesticity, sugar, weed, booze, television, actual porn, believing my own lies.

Why is it so hard to do anything at all, to be anything at all?

My mere existence is an albatross, an anchor, a shouldered world. My breath is quicksand. So sweet to let it pull me under, to die brain-death, soul-death, shadow-death, with pants down and the television on, high, drunk, numb, too inanimate to be sad, too dead to die like a man.

So many people want to say, I AM. Well, are they? Even if my name is not written again after my life span, I am here through my work. What makes me different? I am a Shadow Man, a Shade in the world of light and sun. My destiny is bound with the whole history of humanity. Does a name even matter when my work is alive and flows with all culture backward and forward through time? In every Bardo there is an exchange. When speaking to a Shadow they speak back to me, and they listen. I only need a name if I intend to walk in the light, amongst the people of the sun. Side by side my public side.

I wish I could just walk into to the light, live in the light. I wish I could just give up the ghost. I wish I could eat animal flesh without crying. I wish I could look another person in the eye without feeling the weight of all their suffering, all their experience, and not be overcome with the hopelessness that I can't do anything about it, and they can't alleviate mine either. I wish I could just eat donuts and smoke weed all day watching television and not know deep down that I am doing something wrong, a disservice to myself, to the world, in avoiding my destiny. I wish I could just be happy, not feel as much, not know that all life is suffering, and that everything I do, every move I make will add some suffering to someone, many people, somewhere, no matter how much I am actively working to reduce the suffering of others. I wish my work was not clandestine, not in the shadows, and that walking in the light I could be that light. I want to let go of my dark angel and embrace my radiant goddess. I wish love was enough and that art mattered.

She is an asset, just an asset, I must remind myself. She allows me to walk in the sun, be in the light, to be normal.

I can't love her, because she doesn't understand me, she doesn't know me. I don't let her, I deceive her daily. It can't be any other way. So I can't be any other way.

I don't know how to be home. Home is always an act. I have been on the road, on the run, in the shadows for too long.

Margot and Rudolph Wittkower on the origins of the Saturnine Temperament:

It was Aristotle who first postulated a connection between the melancholic humour and outstanding talent in the arts and science. 'All extraordinary men distinguished in philosophy, politics, poetry, and the arts,' he maintained, 'are evidently melancholic.' Thus he gave rise to the belief in the link between genius and melancholy. But the melancholy of such men is a precarious gift, for if the black bile is not properly tempered, it may produce depression, epilepsy, palsy, lethargy and what we would nowadays call anxiety complexes—in a word, although only the homo melancholicus *can rise to the loftiest heights, he is often prone to conditions bordering on insanity.*

Un livre est un suicide differe.

I counsel myself with Cioran's words:
"The feeling that you cannot survive such whirlwinds also arises from a consummation on a

purely inner plane. The flames of life burn in a closed oven from which the heat cannot escape. Those who live on an external plane [or out in the light, as we would say] are saved from the outset: but do they have anything to save when they are not aware of any danger? The paroxysm of interior experience leads you to regions where danger is absolute, because life which self-consciously actualizes its roots in experience can only negate itself...

"Did not all mystics feel that they could not live after their great ecstasies? What could they expect from this world, those who sense, beyond the normal limits, life loneliness, despair, death?"

Thus is the life of the Shadow Man. Many mystics have been in our ranks.

I love when Brother Cioran posits the question, "Can we imagine a city-dweller who does not have the soul of a murderer?"

Brother Poe would like this sentiment.

Brother Cioran does warn us, "It is not the violent evils that mark us but the secret, insistent tolerable ones belonging to our daily round and undermining us as conscientiously as Time itself."

Before he stepped out of the light he dabbled in despairing doctrines and demagogueries. Our destiny is a difficult one and the tests that it brings us are often failed. Our shame keeps us warm out of the light.

Truer and more constant in the struggle for this world—and she suffered accordingly for it—is Sister Akhmatova. At my darkest, when my demons are dragging me down, down to the blinding depths, I look to her and how she tamed hers, word-whipping them into submission and utility.

To the Death she challenged: "You will come in any case—so why not now?/How long I wait and wait. The bad times fall./I have put out the light and opened the door/for you, because you are simple and magical."

Years later while fighting hard she gave up the ghost a bit:

> *Already madness lifts its wing*
> *to cover half my soul.*
> *That taste of opiate wine!*
> *Lure of the dark valley!*
>
> *Now everything is clear.*
> *I admit my defeat. The tongue*
> *of my ravings in my ear*
> *is the tongue of a stranger.*

And, as his strength
Failed him at length,
He met a pilgrim shadow—
'Shadow,' said he,
'Where can it be—
This land of Eldorado?'

'Over the Mountains
Of the Moon,
Down the Valley of the Shadow,
Ride, boldly ride,'
The shade replied,—
'If you seek for Eldorado!'

Every book is a Shadow Book. Every book has a
Shadow Book. So many books I will not write. Their

titles haunt me. Characters unborn. Statements half uttered, falling down around me. Shadows cast in every direction, darkness upon darkness. The weight is oppressive. I can't breathe. There is more undone than done. More unsaid than said. The temptation not to pass into existence is so strong.

Sometimes I feel like a ghost haunting myself.

Haunting my own life.

I must be an acrobat to talk like this and act like that.

Venice might be my favorite city on Earth. As it continues to sink it nonetheless appears to have risen out of the sea. Brother Nietzsche called it "a symbol for future mankind," and he is more correct year by year. It is a city made up of more profound solitudes than even he could estimate. Ruskin, not a brother, must have been suspicious of us and this connection, as he notes on Venice: "upon the sands of the sea, so weak—so quiet—so bereft of all but her loveliness, that we might well doubt, as we watched her faint reflection in the mirage of the lagoon, which was the City, and which the Shadow."

The Shadow Man is not here to destroy reality, but to complete it.

So many cities, so many people, so many crowds. It is there we are alive, where we feel life teeming and only deep extremes are possible. Brother Benjamin referring to Brother Baudelaire and Brother Poe's description of the crowd reminds us, it is a place "where everything, even horror, turns to magic."

Our message has been betrayed by many. Sad fascist D'Annunzio took our mission away from the inherent compassion of our duty. He thought, "life was a gift from the few to the many, from those who know and have to those who don't know and don't have." We do not look down on the people of the sun. If we thought less of them how and why would and could we do our work?

Some Shadow Men eat their tails until they are consumed with the self and forget the world until there is nothing left. They have put a hole in the world, and they have become that hole.

Sometimes my demon becomes as angel, a dark, dark angel. She kicks me down and holds me there, her tiny, adorable, dark foot, like a spiked boot on my throat. It feels like a brick. A boot, a brick, the metaphor changes with the pain. It grinds me down. So beautiful and delicate it looks. So heavy and rough it feels. I choke, I can't breath, and she smiles down at me. She is an angel, a messenger, a dark messenger. I wake coughing, unable to speak. She is not a dream.

Dark Angel, pull me up to slap me down,
I would lick the hem of your cunt.
Drawing eyes, I turn your scars to frowns.
I want to take my self away from you.

You are the place reserved for the rage in my heart.
Please set me free.

I'd like to write a story called, "Space Hell," and its
gist would be, we know that there is no after-ife
underworld beneath the Earth's crust, but that
doesn't mean the jury isn't still out on Space Hell. We
know that in space no one can hear you scream. There
isn't any wind—the fake moonlanding looked so

bogus. Without sound or air it sounds pretty hellish; you'd be dead so fast. Space ships are just Charon's ferry and if you go too far in any direction, boom, you run right into a star like our sun. Truly hellish.

It has gotten darker. I have gotten darker. The world is always dark, but the Shadow Man can see in the dark as well as the light—better actually. My head hurts, my couch has a permanent crease from my dead weight. The life that I have established here, with her, with all that she involves and contains, requires finding a holistic scenario, a bridge between my work in the shadows and a life in the light with our commitment. There is no halfway in the double life. I can be that Shadow Man, I can walk in the light, for all its hidden dangers and pitfalls oblique. I can do it with a book. *BOMB* is not ready, *BOMB* will never be ready. I must tell a story that hints at giving up the ghost, that entertains and draws a crowd, that walks the line of reality and doubt, truth and desire. This is a tall order. I can do this though, this is what *we* do, but doing it in the light, out in the open for the people of the sun, selling it to them, that is the challenge. She would like it, she needs it for me, it will qualify her expectations.

I can start with the ancient favorite, the battle of opposing forces: small, weak, and righteous against an incomprehensible, large, wicked force. Destiny, situations beyond anyone's control, and the tragic inevitable will have to be there. The picaresque, the spy, the detective, all these facets of our world will translate nicely.

Start with the beginning (a beginning), a foundation of ancient Egypt, some Beowulf, ample Quixote, a dash of Mailer scooped through Burroughs and Matthew Barney, a heaping cup of the inability to avoid the influence of video games and then add all the other accents that will seem like obvious inclusions along the way. The ecstatic madness of Carrington.

We have the holy fool, a plucky and blessed idiot, he has a destiny to assume. Ultimately, he must defeat the Adversary, and before that he must be initiated, he must possess the Secret Name, once he has this name, the game is on. The Adversary will try to kill him, and will succeed unless he finds and kills the Adversary first.

What kind of holy fool should I create? What

would be easy, what is at hand? Where am I? When am I? Let's give it a shot.

I could do it as a fun game, an outward commentary on video game and role playing culture:

Chapter One: The Letter Arrives

We all have a Secret Name. Only the chosen few who reach a world beyond their ordinary lives and circumstances ever learn it. That Secret Name is a deeper, truer part of who you are. Knowing it makes you dangerous and deadly. When you have taken on this Secret Name, this truer identity, you live in a new world of light, a new shade of white light. When you have passed through shadow into dawn-light of new purpose, a world of blood-orange-day, there is but one goal: kill the Adversary.

Everyone has one, but only when the Secret Name is known, your true identity, is the other identity known.

There is no rest in the new dawn until the Adversary is dead. Then there is peace, there is noon, the sun is high and the head of you shines, he of the Secret Name, he with no Adversary.

Landry Bread wanted this life. Who wouldn't? He signed up for it on the Secret Name website seven months ago. You had to wait your turn. There was limited availability and a long wait list. The five hundred dollar deposit was nothing for this opportunity, and the next one thousand sat in a Pay Pal dock refreshed daily, ready to send. To see the world, play this game, would be a dream come true for Landry Bread. He had never left Athens, Georgia. Born here, raised here, he even attended college here, in his own hometown, a college town. Seven months ago he ordered a passport and paid extra for it to be a rush. He knew the Secret Name waitlist would be long, but he couldn't take any chances. He didn't want to be ill-prepared when the calling came.

And so Landry Bread waited. And waited. Seven months of waiting. Every day home from College Copy he checked the mail at the top of the driveway and then went on down to the house. The banality of his job, filling paper trays, making copies, printing books bound in spiral plastic for classes, all led him through the day toward the bus from

Downtown to the East Side to the mile walk from the bus stop to his house at the end of a cul-de-sac and the mailbox at the top of the drive. Seven months of bills, junk mail, catalogs, and over the course of one week, birthday cards for his mother.

Landry Bread lived with his mother, Rosemary. It was her house, not the one he was born in, but only the second he had ever lived in. His parents moved from his birth home to this one while he was in college, during his time in the dorms, an attempt to have a more collegey experience while attending the school in his hometown. This was the house his father died in and returning home after college to live with his mother felt more like a roommate situation. His mother mostly stayed upstairs in her room. She had a television up there, a laptop computer, and a small refrigerator. There was a full bath on that floor too. She only went downstairs to make meals for herself but Landry rarely witnessed this. Everyday he slid her mail under her bedroom door and whatever catalogs he thought she might like. She did most of her shopping online.

It was the greatest moment of happenstance, when Landry Bread discovered the Secret Name website. To play a game, this game, outside of a game console was a dream come true...

But it should be real, within the world of the text, it should be real. Not a global role playing game, real destiny, real tradition back to ancient Egypt and before, real secret name, real adversary, real danger, real commentary, real holy idiot.

I could do it like this:

Chapter One: The Letter Arrives and The Reader Meets Our Hero, Landry Bread, a Young Man at a Precipice

It was the 31st of May when Landry Bread received his calling, the same calling everyone receives at some point in their life, but thankfully for this story and the world, he took it seriously. The day was sunny and it was very hot. None of this was strange; it was Georgia in May. The letter was just sitting in his mailbox with other mail, just like the other mail. It was so much like the other mail that Landry Bread just picked it up with all the mail, as he did every day when he arrived home from work at five. Just picked it all up from the mailbox with his sweaty hands—for all of him was sweaty, having walked a mile from the bus stop to his house—and carried it carefully—but no more carefully than usual—to avoid dripping sweat onto it, into his mother's house where he lived.

Registering quickly that his mother was not in the living room, Landry shouted upstairs that he was home and deposited the mail on the coffee table. In the kitchen, he got a glass of water and drank it down so quickly that a quarter of it made it out of the sides of his mouth and onto his shirt. No bother since it was already wet. Landry wiped a paper towel across his mouth and head and brought it into the living room with a full glass of water. In the living room, he turned on the television and changed channels slowly until he could hear and feel the stereo effect of the same channel his mother was watching upstairs being played in two rooms. He changed to the next channel, somehow reassured to know that she was watching something up there.

On the coffee table he spread out the mail into piles. The circular and coupons going into a pile mentally labeled *Recycling*, and bills for his mother Rosemary and for him going into the same pile mentally labeled *Bills*. All that was left apart from the two distinct piles was the letter. Landry picked it up and put it next him on the couch, but was distracted for a moment by the television. A nature show on Discovery Channel, animals in the wild, and that is where his attention went. He sat back further into the leather couch, shuffling side to side to unstick his thighs from its cling. He reflexively sipped at the water while he watched the program. It was a very ordinary day for Landry.

He woke at 6:45 this morning as usual. He dressed in shorts and a t-shirt and ate cereal. His mother was asleep on the couch in the living room with the television on. He was always careful not to wake her or turn the television off. He took an apple with him and walked on out of the house, out of the cul-de-sac, and up the street to another street, a mile to the bus stop. Along the way he smiled at neighbors out walking their dogs or out running. Some smiled and turned away, some just turned away.

Though he was no longer a student, his college ID worked for free passage onto the bus. He never questioned this, nor did anyone else, this infringement of legality, and he took the bus twice a day. It let him out at campus as if he was a student still and Landry walked across North Campus into Downtown to The Copy Shop. In deft and reflexive movements he said hi to Sherrie and Bill, put on his apron, and inserted his time card into the old green clock-bearing machine on the wall in the break room. A sharp punching stamping sound came down. Then it was a day of Windexing copier screens, loading paper trays, plastic spiral binding packets for classes, some customer service at the register or assisting at a machine, and then sweeping and vacuuming up to close his shift at four. Walk to bus stop, bus, then walk from bus stop to his house. He was home by five every day.

It would be quite doubtful to claim that Landry was waiting for a dare-to-be-great situation. His waiting was not an active process, though he was as always ready for a dare-to-be-great situation as he was ready for any new situation, but none had yet arrived. He worked at The Copy Shop while in college and when he graduated nothing changed. He didn't love his job, but he certainly didn't dislike it. He knew where everything went and he knew how to do everything there that needed to be done. He trained new hires and was a reliable worker in every way necessary. His closest friends in high school went away to college. His closest college friends went away back home or off for jobs after graduation. Back then

Landry was apprehensive about leaving his mother alone, today he will have no trouble with the decision.

He played bar trivia with some people from work and their friends. Some co-workers and friends of co-workers, not even friends and friends of friends. That was every Tuesday and Thursday. Sometimes he went out to hear bands on a Friday or Saturday night, but that was all contingent on invitations from co-workers. Often he would see some pretty cool-looking people in The Copy Shop making fliers and posters for their band's show. These marketing devices often intrigued him, the arty images the bands employed and the strange names. The flyers and posters were public announcements, telling anyone, any stranger on the street, to go see that band play at a particular venue at a particular time and date, and yet Landry always viewed them with apprehension, as only the first part of a suggestion. The second part, the deal-sealing part, only came if a co-worker made some indication of a featured band being worth seeing and of possibly going. It was not so much that Landry's trepidation at life was born out of wisdom, but he was more so a follower out of habit. And all habits can be broken.

Until today, no one would have ever considered Landry Bread a lucky person. But there it was, a hand-addressed envelope with no return address and no postage or postal stamp, the key to Landry Bread's destiny and essential role in preserving civilization as we know it today, and it was sitting on his coffee table next to the couch on which he slumped watching one animal devour another on the television.

Eventually I will get him off that couch. Eventually he will open the letter. He will see handwritten instructions in beautiful calligraphy. He will see the word destiny. It will excite him. Something slumbering inside of him will wake, just a little, but its deep reverberations will ripple through every part of his being.

He will read it all again. And he will read it all again. Such a short and precisely written letter. Perfectly suited for his Landry Bread nature, we will believe it all. He will have no doubt that he should follow the instructions. That night he will lie in bed, having entered it at the same time he did every night, and through his mind will run the lines from his favorite childhood movie, *Find and fulfill your destiny...* *find and fulfill your destiny...* The breathy voice of Laurence Olivier. *Find and fulfill your destiny...* And he will drift off to sleep smiling wide...

Chapter Two is easy, no matter how Chapter One ends up:

Chapter Two: In the Portal, Learning Traveling, Learning Spanish, and Meeting, Not a Ninja, but a Ghost

The airport. Oh, the airport. What a treat for Landry Bread. He hasn't been here since a senior-year-trip to Mexico. That was also the first, last, and only time he ever used his passport. It is quite lucky he has one actually—likely more than luck. Now at this age he is a little more open to the sacred power and mystery of this place. Airports are portals, that much is obvious. You pop in, do what you are told, follow the queue, move through the channels, wait, move on, sit, wait, do what you are told, stand, follow the channels, queue some more, sit, do what you are told, stand, queue follow the channels and you are out, out in a very different location. Of course, entry into the portal, beyond the most superficial anteroom, is contingent on the right paper work, documents of authority with their own sacred power and mystery. But once obtained and access to the portal is established, this place that touches all places reveals its true power, a power lost on many—or even invisible to those it does not affect—and hence mysterious. An airport is a portal and a place of transformation. As a portal of transformation it acts in the most ritualistic fashion. You ask to enter, some times less consciously than others. Sometimes the asking comes with great labors of work for the cost. Sometimes you are called. But you always ask to enter.

Once entered, the portal contains trails of its own, subtle challenges and the never-blinking eye of authority beyond your understanding. The airport is the liminal space. It serves for people in Landry's time like the Bardo of the ancient Buddhists, that space between lives or merely between moments of true consciousness and a return back into the dirty world of suffering and ignorance. Heidegger in his ham-fisted way described this as Dasein and of course he laughably thought Hitler was the Absolute. The airport is more than just a time-out; it is a real transformation of the identity. Your transcendentalist is wrong, Landry Bread in Georgia is actually very different from Landry Bread in Spain and everywhere else he goes, that you will soon see. Actually your transcendentalist was half right. Travel is a fool's paradise, but it is a paradise for holy fools. Strange for a transcendentalist to overlook the holy. But regardless, where were we in our story? Or should I say, where is Landry Bread in our story?

The airport. Landry made it from the shuttle to the signs indicating his airline. The right channel led him to the counter where he bought a ticket fortuitously for the last seat left on the flight. He paid with his debit card and a smile. No flags went up as his bank-sanctioned purchase laid his identity bare before the unblinking authoritarian eye of the portal. The blonde counter attendant of the airline, with tan skin and a Spanish accent, asked Mr. Bread if he had any bags to check. Her tone was kind—and possibly regardless of the fact that Landry had just purchased by debit card a $2,200 business class ticket—and if she were to take him by the hand, Landry would have followed anywhere. He especially liked being called

Mr. Bread, and her eyes, and her breasts, from what he could glimpse.

"I have this bag. Should I check it?"

And he went through the trouble of slipping his arms backwards out of the loops and taking his backpack off, extending it to her.

"You could check that, Sir, but a bag that size is within carry-on limits. Perhaps you might need items within during your flight."

As she didn't reach out to touch it he lowered his arms.

"Your flight begins boarding at 6:30 at Gate D-23. Just take the tram to Terminal D and wait at Gate number 23 there. Have a lovely flight, Mr. Bread."

There it was again, a beautiful woman with beautiful eyes and beautiful breasts, from what he could tell, saying his formal name in an accent. He did exactly as she told him.

Now he sits on the end seat on a bench directly under the gray sign reading white characters D-23. He is leaning forward, his backpack making him wider going back. He is in awe of this place. So many strange people. So many pretty people. So many people of different shades of tan, brown, and black. So many people of sizes to both extremes. A constant flow moving in both directions up and down the aisle, stamping by in groups, individuals or couples running, the flow interrupted by someone who stands to read the paper in his hands and look up and back down to paper before moving back into the flow of the channel.

Landry sits forward because of his backpack but also because his feet are poised on their balls with his calves taut. He rocks on the roll of the balls.

I am a traveler, I am a traveler, I am doing it, I am going, like him, like her, like them, I am doing it, I am going, Landry whispers softly to himself. Already he is changing. But how to change? This is what he is thinking.

How do I be like them, how do I do it? I did what the woman told me to do, but that just got me in. I am not like them. They are so assured, packed, walking, reading the different papers in their hands. Even the sitting people look so comfortable, relaxed, prepared, reading books and magazines. I need to blend. I need to gear up. I need to rise to the occasion. To find and fulfill my destiny. To find my secret name. I need to be a traveler.

He takes his backpack off and puts it by his feet like the person sitting closest to him, a brown-skinned man with longish brown hair wearing a blue collared shirt and a tan blazer. Landry is wearing a t-shirt, as other people are too, but none still had their backpacks on. Observing the crowd at Gate D-23, two hours before the boarding time, one of the most common traits he notices is that everyone is so relaxed in their travel experience that they are busy doing something else. They are reading books and magazines, playing on laptops or smartphones, texting or just talking to one another. Landry was alone and had packed his backpack as if he were going to a long slumber party. He had clothes and toiletries. He can't sit here like this and be a traveler.

Landry rises, replaces his pack and moves into the flow of foot traffic. As he veers off with the current from the gate the lady sent him to he looks back at it over his shoulder, at his seat, at the Gate sign above it, at his seat, and then turns back giving himself up to the flow of the current.

Most of the people around him seem bent on a great distance, to the escalators from flights just landed. Others, he understood, were just being good residents of the Terminal, getting food, stretching legs, breaking out of the channel of others with purpose. These are the others he needs to emulate. He thinks of them as locals and as a new traveler he is trying to go local. Landry makes his break out of the channel to a newsstand bookstore. Supplies, all of the traveler's needs here, things he didn't realize he would need, but that's what learning is all about, he thinks, realizing things he didn't think he would need.

The travel magazine section excites and confuses him at the same time. So many titles with so many photo covers of locations where you should go surrounded by the words of more locations telling you where to go. But Landry realizes that he knows where he is going, he has the ticket already, he has achieved passage into the portal. He is locked in with no choice but to follow, but to follow the crowd at his gate at the time like the woman told him and to arrive in Spain. So what did these magazines serve? From the covers none were of Spain. What was a traveler to read by way of magazine if his destination was not featured? He could read of other places to go. That must be the culture of travelers that he needs to understand and feel, the motion. That was it. That was what he felt since he entered. This place was bottled tension and pressurized with motion. The streams of foot traffic he watched in the aisles were like bubbles in a Coke bottle swirling around waiting for their chance to get out but by nature could not be still. Some sat and read or texted or watched, but they were all pressurized in that they were ready at all times for their new location. The magazines showed that even on the way to a new location they were always thinking about or preparing for a newer location. Landry suspects that the excitement he feels is this excitement of a traveler. Greece, among ruins and sunny beaches;

Antarctica, crisp ice, blue water, boats, coats, penguins; Thailand, all jungle and pointy gold Buddha-things; even Branson, Missouri with bright lights, the Las Vegas of country music; a new newer destination in here, each magazine says to him and out there through each gate he knows they call in their own voices.

But he is going to Spain and he doesn't have to decide if he is a Budget, Conde, Leisure, or Frommer's traveler, so instead he moves farther down the selections to books. Here he finds Spain. Here he realizes that he might just be a Frommer's, it jumps out the biggest at him. A fat book. A sharp-chinned woman in festive dress spinning in dance. Spain, so big and white on a red background. This is for the serious traveler with a real destination. Not for reading travel news and dabbling in thoughts of other destinations. This book is heavy in his hand and he understands it is through this work that he can know Spain, a confident traveler knowing where he is going. He is sure of his purchase and feeling more excited. This buy will make him more real. What should the next buy do?

The next buy is from a selection of smaller books Landry finds adjacent to the travel guides. The section says language books. The Spanish speak Spanish, that is a given. Landry took two semesters of

French in high school. Mostly he remembers jokes about cognates. The French word for croissant is *croissant*, the French way to say bon voyage is *bon voyage*, and so forth. The book he draws is lighter in his hands, but he is sold on the brand, it calls to him from a smaller cover in the same white on red and it bears a different spinning woman of festive dress. They are compatible, he has a set, but what else, what else? What else could he need, what else is everyone else buying? What goes in a traveler's pack? He must gear-up. The notion from so many movies bubbles his excitement beyond his containable brim. He can't focus.

Landry needs guidance. He asks the woman at the register. She is brown and sharp-chinned, eyebrows drawn in unmovable arches, hair long down her back; and she is Indian: dots not feather, it is a reflex of thought. But she has the supplies, she knows the travelers, sees them every day, all day. She might even be a traveler, maybe she gets discounts on tickets from working here?

"Excuse me, ma'am. I would like these two books, but I was wondering if there is anything else you would recommend for a traveler on his way to Spain. I am going to Spain at 6:30 at Gate D-23. I am sure I need more than these two books, I just don't know what."

He smiled.

She smiled.

"Spain? That is in Europe. Will you be plugging in things? You know, into the wall?

"Maybe. I guess. I hope so."

"Well, then you will need a converter. We have them. They're there."

Her accent is thick, but he follows a line for direction from her brown finger to the wall. The wall is full of many small plastic apparatuses and a world of other supplies.

"I don't know what to choose."

"Take the universal one. In case you go somewhere else other than Europe. It will work wherever you go."

That is exactly what he wants and he quickly hones in on a futuristic-looking object, a twisted plastic ball with spikes of different shapes, a talisman of a new world, which reads *Universal Converter.*

"Anything else?" he almost shouts across the aisle that separates him from the counter and then her.

"Uhm. Chewing gum?"

"Chewing gum!"

"Yes, we have it here." She points down in front of her to the rows of chewing gum.

Landry grabs one pack from each box on the

top row and puts it all down with the converter on the books. He smiles at her and she smiles back and begins to ring him up. He hands her his debit card and then starts to look around at the long line that has formed down the aisles past the magazines of other customers, holding various items, some like his, and shuffling their feet. Landry smiles widely at them, a satisfied traveler smiling at other travelers, and to his satisfaction they all smile back at him.

*

After returning to his seat, right under the Gate D-23 sign and somehow the only seat in the section not occupied, Landry comes to the conclusion that he must learn Spanish as soon as possible. The woman who sold him his ticket is now at the counter of the airline at the boarding zone. She is beautiful, and the more he stares at her and then back down at the different women on the books he bought, the more he thinks that if these women pictured are Spanish, then that woman must be too. She had an accent; it was a strong part of her beauty. *Mister Bread*, she said. It rolled so smooth and warm out of her. And she said it in English. A real traveler would speak the language of where he goes. The plane is a place between here and there. His most logical summation is that the plane is at least half here and half there.

Landry Bread figures he has about an hour to

learn Spanish. He will look into the travel guide of Spain on the flight. Now he must work. Gear up his mind. At the bottom of the book's cover reads a subtitle, *Real Language for Travelers*, and his confidence is made more solid. He goes in. A table of contents, looks good, looks like necessary stuff. An introduction on how to use the book and then words. English, then bold in Spanish and italicized pronunciation keys. He flips to the back, not even 300 pages. See the word in English, see it in Spanish, learn how to pronounce it. Maybe I can learn Spanish in the next couple hours, at least most of it, the important travel stuff?

Landry goes for it. He tries out greetings in his head, peruses the airport-specific stuff, jumps around to the later lessons to see how hard they get. With each word and each phrase, easily pronounceable with the key, his confidence builds. He is a traveler learning the real language for travelers. Soon it's too much to hold it in any longer.

"Hola! Como esta? Me llamo Landry Pan," he says to the man sitting directly to his left.

"Seriously, bro, your name is Landry Pan? Is that like Peter Pan? Are you his American brother? Are you flying off from here to fight some pirates? Shouldn't you be singing about it?" says the man, not much older than him.

Landry is taken aback and in a strange

confusion. He said everything correctly, and he was understood, but not entirely.

"Pan is Spanish for bread," he squeaks out, clarifying.

"True, true, that is true, bro. Pan is Spanish for bread. Are you trying to tell me that your name is Landry Bread?"

"Yes, Landry Bread."

"Oohhh, alright. But you don't have to translate every word just cause you can. Especially not your name."

"Okay."

"Hah. Landry Bread. And how'd you know I speak Spanish, anyway? Cause I'm brown, I gotta be Mexican or something, not speaka no ingleeesh?" He comes on so tough, a young brown man with a goatee and cornrows braided back in his hair, loose hoodie and baggy pants. Regardless, the over-affected accent is enough make Landry smile.

"You are sitting at Gate D-23. It is going to Spain. Shouldn't everyone going to Spain be able to speak Spanish? I am learning right now."

"Hah, that's a good point. My man, Landry. Actually, I am going to Portugal, I change planes in Madrid, but I learned Spanish when I was a kid. My grandmother made me learn. Not my Grams, she was black, and not interested at all in speaking any other language but English in her own way. It was my Abuelita that made me learn. That's Spanish for grandmother, but really it's like little grandmother, it's sweeter that way. She was from Puerto Rico, like my Pops."

"Ah-bue-li-ta."

"That's it, you're getting it, Landry-man. You can actually get away with calling any old lady Abuelita, they'll instantly love you and treat you like their own grandkid. Maybe give you a hard candy or ginger snap or churro or whatever shit they have over there. So, Landry Bread, not Landry Pan, a man with a very short familiarity with the Spanish language, but getting on a plane at Gate D-23 to Spain nonetheless, why are you going to Spain?"

"I am going to find my secret name. It is at the west entrance to the Prado in Madrid. I have a letter."

The brown face stares hard at Landry. The left eyebrow rises high and arched. The neck cranes a couple of inches closer and stares harder. Then the whole face bursts out with laughter, the hoodie jiggles exaggeratedly and he slaps his knee.

"Man, you're serious aren't you? I know you are. Landry-man. You are great. 'Me llamo Landry Pan.' Shit. I dig that, man. I dig you. So you are going to find your secret name? And it is just waiting for you at the west gate entrance of the Prado in Madrid. Man,

I know you will. Do you know that? I totally believe you will. Landry Bread is gonna find his secret name. Alright. Well, it seems you have some mission ahead of you. I am glad to meet you. I'm Arty Cienfuegos."

"I am glad to meet you too, Arty Cienfuegos." Landry extends his hand and Arty shakes it.

"Now, Arty is short for Arturo, and that is Spanish, but I don't think it means anything. It is just like the Spanish version of Arthur. But my last name does mean something, you don't have to translate it, just keep it in Spanish, but you can learn a little more Spanish here with it. Cienfuegos means one hundred fires, and I got no idea where it comes from. Maybe my great-great-great grandfather was a pyro or something."

"Cien fuegos. One hundred fires."

"That's it. How long you been studying Spanish?"

"Almost an hour." And as Arty laughs, Landry realizes that part of being a traveler is to hold his own in the traveler exchange. "Why are you going to Madrid to go to Portugal, Arty?"

"Oh, man, Madrid is just a layover to change planes. But I am just going to Portugal, to travel, to backpack, to see the world, and that is the first place geographically in Europe, the farthest west, so I am starting there. From there it is everywhere."

"From there it is everywhere," Landry whispers to himself, his eyes going wide fast.

"Yeah man, everywhere. I'm gonna hit all the capitals and beaches and every church and monument and battlefield and crazy discotheque rave dance party Europe throws my way, bump in every club. And then after that, you know what?"

"What?"

"Then I am gonna hit Asia, maybe some Africa too, but Asia, man. Backpacking Thailand, Vietnam, Cambodia, Phnom Penh in monsoon season, maybe a train across China and Siberia or out to Indonesia, Malaysia, more beach, learn some surfing, and ladies of all skin shades. It all starts with this flight here we are waiting for."

"Wow, you must be a real traveler," says Landry, in awe that he has met a real traveler with all the zeal, excitement, and knowledge that he wants.

"I am about to be. I just been saving for a while, shit, for a long time, saving in every crazy way possible. I been ghosting, living like a ghost for so long with the most minimal overhead possible while temping and making some mad hourly dollar that this dream of the world is about to come true."

"What is *ghosting*?" More wonder from Landry Bread, a willing pupil before a teacher.

"Ghosting? Man, Landry-man, it's a whole

'nother world. Living like a ghost. My way of life for the last two years. I have been temping all over Atlanta, making like twelve bucks an hour, fifteen bucks an hour, sometimes even eighteen bucks an hour, and my official mailing address for the last two years has been a P.O. Box. So the idea is, I work and save and try to live with no overhead. As little overhead as possible. And I did it. I am gonna see the world. And ghosting made it a much quicker return. But ghosting ain't entirely legal, you understand. Not legal at all."

"What is *ghosting*?" Landry asks again.

"I am getting there. You see. I reduce overhead in a big city like Atlanta, or even more so if you ghost somewhere like Chicago or New York or San Francisco, like some of the guys did who taught me. My legal address is the P.O. Box, and where you sleep and live is where the ghost skills come in. I was taught by this guy, Lazarus. I don't even think he worked, just ghosted. 'Work is for young ghosts, little g's starting out. I'm retired on the only thing I have, my skills,' he told me. I met him through some deejay friends in Atlanta that were already ghosting. They pretty much told me how to do it, what it was all about, but Lazarus let me in on the art involved.

"What you do is—and this is the illegal part, the part that makes the whole thing illegal—you break into someone's house when they are out of town. How do you know when they are out of town? How do you know when they are coming back? That is all part of various ghosting skills, or prep-work. It is also that part that makes Lazarus so unbelievable now, how good he is, not working and all. I would pick people based on where I worked. When temping you need to always be listening. Most people just talk all day at work, about nothing, everything, about shit. Most people just ignore the temps too. I learned who was going out of town, when, and for how long. They just said it out loud. And the address, well that's just in their file, and filing is mostly what temps do.

"The prep-work is key, and it isn't easy; you gotta be careful. Gotta case the place too. Houses aren't good, apartments are best, and the bigger the building the better. Door placement is also a big deal. So, all that done, you got a place picked, this is where the ghost work comes in. You break in. You pick the lock. I got pretty good. You need a little kit for it, but I left mine with a friend. It is too risky to travel with it. Or you slip the window lock, or just bust the door, window, screen, whatever. Then—and here is where the art of the ghost begins—you fix it. Screens are easy to replace, so are locks, windows less so. But it is best to get in without any damage. When you are in you instantly get out one of these."

Arty draws a silver digital camera from his hoodie pocket.

"As essential for ghosting as for seeing the world," he says.

"I need one of those. I need to get one," laments Landry.

"Yeah man, they'll have one in Spain. But this is a ghost's main weapon. You get in that apartment and start snapping away. Everything. Like everything. Bookshelves, picture frames, knick-knacks, cabinets, cabinet shelves, refrigerator shelves, coffee table books—were they at ninety-degree angles or at diagonals? You have that whole entire house just like the people who live there left it in your camera. Everything so you can entirely reconstruct the scene if you need to. Lazarus told me how in the days before digital cameras it was all Polaroids, and ghosts were carrying around stacks of them. That shit must have been expensive. Even before the Polaroids it was just drawings and memories. You got into the house and started sketching. Lazarus claimed to have skills predating all of that. He did it all by memory, photographic memory. That is just crazy to me. I live and swear by this little camera. I mean I take notes too and work on the memory, but that is a lot of trust on the memory, especially one as old as Lazarus's. Either way, once the documentation is perfect, then you start living. It is your place now.

"There are particular rules depending on the particular place. Some situations are better than others. If there are too many windows letting out to close apartments, you gotta keep the blinds and drapes closed and use little light. Those aren't good situations, and you should've picked up on that in your prep-work. You also avoid places with pets or too many plants since they are the ones who will need people to stop in and pet sit or water the plants. That's all part of the prep-work. The best situations have no or few windows, or windows that let out to trees or walls or nothing, and then you just keep that tv volume low and just live there. Be sure to note the channel it was on when you got there.

"When the time is up for the family to come home, I usually leave a day early, in case they come home early. I consult my camera and my notes and return everything back to the way it was. I always bring in my own food and take my own trash out with me. A pro-ghost like I became usually has the next house prepped and ready and just slides over to that one when one is up. Sometimes I have even worn clothes from a house I was ghosting to a job interview for another temp gig. I like to move out of one job after ghosting a co-worker. But sometimes it is fun to just hang around them at the office after I lived in their house and slept in their bed. It is like nothing ever happened. But you see, Landry-man, that is the whole idea of ghosting. It *is* like nothing ever happened. They never know I was there. I live free with no rent, no utilities, no cable bill, no renting movies or buying books, and they never know they just shared their life and all their stuff with me. As far as they know, I was never there. I am a ghost. I think they can feel it though, I think deep down they really know, inexplicably know. And that is why it is even more like a ghost. They feel that someone has been there, but everything is in the exact place they left it. How can that be? It makes no sense. Still they can feel me, the lingering presence of another being. It is scary shit man, just how connected we really are. Even I know that feeling. I look back to being younger and coming home to an empty house and just having that *feeling*, that someone else has been there. And now I wonder, what was that, did someone ghost my house?

"It sounds more like a ninja than a ghost," says Landry.

"I know what you're saying, but there is a big difference. Ninjas are on a mission. Ninjas take something. That is usually what their mission is about, to take an object, or some information, or a life. A ghost takes nothing but the space, and a ghost leaves the space there when he leaves. A ghost haunts the house when you are gone, and a ghost is peaceful. In some ways a ghost is doing a service. The house is safe. No ninjas are getting in to take anything when the ghost is there. When the ghost is gone, everything is left exactly how it was when the people who live there left. A ghost does no harm, just passes through."

"It still sounds a little like a ninja. They are the model of stealthy."

"Okay, okay, but there is always proof that a ninja was there, something is missing, someone is dead. But a ghost, a ghost just leaves a feeling and otherwise your home is perfectly fine. And while the feeling of the ghost might be there when you are home, the ghost himself never will be. Can't say that about a ninja, they come in even when you are home.

"Listen, cool as ninjas sound, ghosts take making your way in this world to a whole 'nother level. Part of making your way in this world is as much about letting people know you are not here as it is about letting them know you are here. Know what I mean?"

"No."

"Alright, Landry-man. I might just be like a year or two older than you, but I really learned something in all of this. You only have so much control in this world, but it is far more than you think. Living like a ghost I felt almost supernatural. I can let the world know when I want it to see me. All 'hello sir, good morning ma'am, here is that file you were looking for, I just made a fresh pot of coffee.' Well dressed, not too urban or ethnic for them, not too scary. And then after hours I am a ghost. No one knows where I am unless I want to tell them. I can live in someone's home for two weeks and they never know I was there. It might not sound like much, but it is power, and it is real."

"I think I understand. I just met my first, not a ninja, but a ghost world traveler," says Landry."

"Yeah, Landry-man, that's it. Maybe we will see some of the world together, after you're done in Spain getting your secret name."

"OH!" and Landry stands up as boarding is called out for his flight. It pulls him out of his seat with purpose like a true traveler and he responds to the calling. Arty rises but lingers.

"C'mon Arty, it is our flight," Landry nags excitedly as he walks to where other walk. Arty hangs back by the seats.

"Sorry, Landry-man, I'm sitting farther back. This boarding is for First and Business Classes, that's what you got so go ahead. I'll make the flight, I just won't be sitting near you."

Landry smiles and looks back and Arty smiles and laughs at his new friend. The tide of people is taking Landry and he is letting it. The order of the portal applies to him as a traveler. He moves to where he is told, he does what he is told, he shows the paper he holds, he shows his passport, he queues farther, he stops. Down a tube he is sent, queuing with others until the plane is in sight and it is just another tube with more rules to take him to another location.

Chapter Three: Bon Voyage, Business Class Traveler, and Some Snakes Enter the Garden

Up above it all, higher than he'd ever flown. By almost every possible human standard of luxury, Landry Bread is comfortable. He is enjoying all the creature comforts of the modern world. And yet he is as restless as a child, with his head whipping around in all directions and both hands and feet fiddling with everything fiddle-with-able in the range of their domain. He is conscious of his own excitement and trying to experience the new world within his reach without drawing attention, but he ultimately does not know how to act on a plane. In business class. On his way to Europe.

Before the plane even took off he was offered champagne or orange juice. He took the orange juice and then as he drank it he regretted not getting the champagne. But he wanted orange juice. But champagne is the kind of thing the people around him would drink. The woman to his right took some. But these are the kind of travelers that take what they want, not something just because it is free. He finished deliberating positively and relaxed a little as he drank his orange juice.

He relaxed a little more after figuring out how the television console comes out of the armrest on his right, how by touching the screen he has the ability to choose from movies, tv shows, video games, and music. And learning how the footrest comes up from below and which button makes the seat go back and what the options for dinner and breakfast are from the menu the flight attendant handed him.

Finally, in the air, he was able to reach that next plateau of relaxation required. Employing the friendliness of his nature and allowing the excitement of his new experience to express itself, he spoke to the woman sitting next to him. The introduction was easy.

"Away we go," he beams as the plane reaches the peak of its height.

The woman laughs. It is a sweet sincere laugh and there is the natural setup to interaction allowing Landry to fully relax into his flight.

"This is only my second flight. The first one was many years ago and much shorter. Not shorter than this flight so far, but shorter than this flight will eventually be, when that happens and we land and it is over. Then it will have been longer. But knowing it will be longer makes this one so much more exciting than the shorter one I had once before. Though it was longer than this one so far."

"Let me stop you there," she says and laughs again. "It seems you might be caught in a loop. I understand what you're saying. I remember my first long flight. It was many more years ago than yours, but I still remember it well. It was a fourteen-hour flight from Seoul to Chicago and I had a window seat like you. Not as nice a seat, not business class, but I made the seat my whole world with my dolls and a blanket."

As she tells her story, the whole story becomes her world again, just within her eyes. Landry is excited to listen and be taken away by her. He likes the idea of a seat fort on a flight but presently feels too big. He wishes he had flown as a child, to have an experience like she expressed.

And since she shared, he shares.

"I'm going to find my secret name," and he beams at her. Within the plane, the section, and then the same two-seat row they are narrowed down together and instantly Landry is feeling like this well-dressed and slight-framed, very attractive, middle-aged Korean woman is his traveling partner. She had wrapped herself up in the airline's blanket in her seat, her legs drawn up, and only her shimmering, stockinged-feet exposed out the bottom of the blanket. When her feet elegantly rubbed against each other in subtle stretches, they caught his eye, and he caught more of her legs, some ankle and calf. Her perfume smelled of wealth and citrus.

"Oh are you now?" she smiles and sips from her champagne. The invisible movements under her blanket read out that she is getting more comfortable, as if for a story, and yet one little shimmery foot remains crossed elegantly over the other. Her smile reads out: tell me more.

"It's true. I will find my true destiny after I get my secret name. I have to go to the Prado. That's in Madrid, Spain. It's a big museum, and at the west entrance someone will give me my secret name. Then comes my destiny. You said you have been traveling a long time. And you look like you have reached your destiny. Have you learned your secret name?" While he speaks, Landry is made even more comfortable by the woman's age. She is likely twenty years older than him, somewhere in her mid-forties, and though she looks nothing like his mother—half the size, elegant to a level he had never experienced, and of course, Korean—he is able to cultivate the tiniest maternal emanation coming from her. She is listening with a motherly interest. However, with another movement of her delicate feet against each other, he realizes in a quick flash that he also finds her attractive. He wants to cuddle under that blanket with her in two very distinct and, until now, oppositional, ways. Oh, the new adventures he was having. Her speaking makes him no less entranced.

"No, just the one public name, Ji-Na Sun Li. But there is something there that does sounds familiar. And you are right, I have been traveling a long time and I've heard of many things. It sounds almost Egyptian. And it sounds like a game. Does it involve another soul or an adversary, maybe?" Her voice had become more professional, with a growing tone of seriousness.

"I don't know. I just have this letter." He shows it to her. She looks at it, reads it, flips it over.

"So you're Landry Bread?" she states more

than asks.

"Yes, do you know me?"

"No, I'm just marveling at your name. It's a good name, I'm Ji-Na," and she offers her small smooth hand into his and he can feel and smell a lotion that confuses his senses and makes him think of a very beautiful wedding cake that he wants to look at and smell but not eat. "I know you now, but this whole things seems to have you very wide-eyed. If there is anything to this we probably shouldn't be talking about it here."

"Why not here?" He says and looks around. "Most people are asleep and the ones awake don't seem interested in us."

"Whatever this is, it has secret in its name and it's always a good idea to refrain from talking secrets here. It has been known that the CIA bugs the first and business class sections of many international flights. They could be listening right now," and her voice got lower and with a tone of a new seriousness.

Landry's head lowers with her voice and his widening eyes look side to side and up around.

"Aren't they the good guys? Maybe if they are listening they can help me? What I'm doing seems like the kind of thing spies would be good at."

"You are friendly, Landry, but this world isn't. Actually, let me amend that a bit. The world is actually friendly, but you might not know what it is beneath that surface, why it is being friendly. For the most part, for most average people living their lives in your country, the CIA is the good guys. But for you out here abroad, on this crazy quest that involves who knows what, you run the risk of being somehow in the middle of something you know nothing about, and maybe in their way. The second you are an obstacle, no matter how small, you will be treated accordingly. Your country doesn't like obstacles, and it is quick these days to label anyone a threat. National security is supreme and you don't want to be on the wrong side of it. On the wrong side you lose personhood."

Her voice had grown lower, smoother, and yet sharper, and her words went right into Landry's mind as if he wasn't actually hearing them, but learning them, or had always known them; they were just there. Her posture changed as she spoke, too. Invisibly, beneath the blanket her spine straightened up against the back of the seat and her left leg crossed the right, its foot now pointing into his legroom, a toe just beyond his armrest.

Landry didn't really understand her, but the words were now thoughts within him. He was experiencing fear for the first time on this adventure, a tiny ember of fear burning in the back of his stomach. And her foot, so close to him, pulled his mind into a different direction. He wanted to touch her foot: the instep, the ankle, then above. He wanted to kiss her thin taupe lips. He wanted her to hold him, to be bigger than him. All these urges surged in his blood and the ember burned with them. There were so many snakes in his garden. Snakes like on the head of Medusa that Perseus would lop then wield. *Find and fulfill...*

"I'm gonna do it!" he says, and smiles proudly.

Ji-Na relaxes everywhere: under the blanket her spine, her eyes and the lines of her mouth, the poised foot. In a new, or returned tone, she asks him, "What?"

This is such a strange craft. Items go in and out of realities. Clearly, I am ripping part of her name and ominous backstory off the Korean woman in the television show, *Lost*. From this reality into that. But it goes both ways. Her foot has come back into my reality, the leg and more. I can see up her thigh through my words constructing that reality. I can feel the arousal and excitement, the very real erection emerging as I write the tops of her stockings. Are they real? Am I? Are you?

Do writers of erotica dream of fucking their characters? Do all writers dream of fucking their characters? They are in you and out from you. And they come out of the world into you. When I close my eyes my characters are as real as my memories and the thoughts of my loved ones. Supposedly, Brother Balzac called out for some of his characters by name on his deathbed.

Brother Fanon reminds us that, "the imaginary life cannot be isolated from real life, the concrete and objective world constantly feed, permit, legitimate, and found the imaginary. The imaginary consciousness is obviously unreal but it feeds on the concrete world. The imagination and the imaginary are possible only to the extent that the real world belongs to us."

I am not sure of how Landry Bread will answer Ji-Na.

He might be ready to kiss her, but he is certainly ready to find and fulfill his destiny. I guess that's the real answer. He wants it, the Secret Name, the name of the Adversary, the completion of a cosmic order with his place defined within it. Chapter Four will see him in Spain's capital, trying to figure his way around and preparing for the next day of going to the Prado, the side entrance, and finding another clue to move him and our story further along, painting portraits of the contemporary world of the traveller, the international, the cosmopolitan.

That first night, after finding a cheap hotel, not far from Madrid's Atocha, the main train station, Landry will venture out into a bar and drink too much, slipping from a bar stool. A tall black man will help him up. Landry asks the man if he is a pirate.

"What, since I am Somali, I must be a pirate?"

"No, I meant like Johnny Depp, Disney, Captain Morgan, pirates from days gone by. Your earring and bandana and roguish twinkling eye," says Landry.

"Ha Ha Ha! I know very much what you meant, my friend. I was only having some sport with you. How could you even know I was from Somalia? Now lets get you cleaned up and get you another drink... So, roguish twinkle in the eye, ay, huh?" says the Somali.

Their conversation will continue into the man explaining about his job in Mogadishu, the presence of Al-Qaeda and Al-Shabaab. The presence of the CIA and MI-6, and the economy for shop-owners like himself (sporting goods, mostly soccer) in sitting between the sides, or running "False Flag" operations.

Landry's mind is blown from all the information and the ubiquity of duplicity in this world, but mostly he enjoys the Somali's accent, and pirate-like roguishness. They drink into the night and out into the streets.

The next morning Landry will wake up with a new book in his presence. He will remember that the Somali gave it to him and told him that it was the biggest book in Europe at the time; that Landry needed to read it to understand the world better. The Somali was going to be bringing another copy home with him, maybe Xerox some copies of his own for his countryman, the kids especially, the ones that could read. Maybe he will sit there in his shop, amongst the hanging jerseys of CECAFA (Central and East African league) teams, and read the book to the kids who hangout on his sidewalk, the street rats who are nothing but eyes and ears (and of course, quick hands), many of whom equally report to Al-Shabaab and Al-Qaeda as to him, whom they would never expect to be on a CIA and MI-6 payroll; but he is.

Landry will find his way to the Prado and while waiting for it to open, sit at a café and read. I need to write this chapter, I can see it, taste it, and it is just out of reach.

And yet nothing has been easier for me than writing Chapter Five, folding in the book within the book:

Chapter 5: The Book, Its Author, and The Spell It Put Its Reader Under

This is what Landry Bread learned from the back of the book, while sitting at a table with coffee outside a café. It was written by a man named Maawaam. He is a French Algerian who was educated at a school in Southern California. That was all anyone knew about him, all his publisher claimed to know. There was a note that some believed his name might be an anagram, more than just a palindrome. It further read: "The debut novel from 'The Banksy of literature,' (Guardian UK) is rocking Europe. *Amerika the Beautifuk* accounts a dark vision of America in the near future where battles rage between a militant police force and bands of anarchist street youths. This controversial criticism of American values and legality gone too far has been hailed as '*A Clockwork Orange* meets *Grapes of Wrath*' (BBC) and 'a critical science fiction vision of America in the future to make Philip K. Dick blush' (Guardian UK).

Knowing all of the references from his time in college, Landry was even more excited to trust the in-person recommendation he already had. His impression of America, his home, had always been pretty positive, never controversial or dark, but those are things that he knew made for good books. *Amerika the Beautifuk*, began *in media res*, another feature of good books that easily excited him:

From where they were they were able to watch the new killer tires on the patrol car just roll through the alley crushing bottles and bricks, the shards like nothing, grinding it all down, and they were next if they didn't stay low, the searchlight scanning waist-high. An angry eye, its cold anger passively discriminate. What it found, it would deal with. Like those new killer tires.

Zero, Zuchero, Tony, and Raerae plastered to the cracks in the alley and pushed low in their breathing. They had woven into the trash, elbows in plastic bags, feet and heads stuck into boxes with found cracks to peek out through. If the pigs had dogs all they would smell was trash. Tongue clicks were all they needed, tongue clicks from each to say the car passed—but the farthest ahead, Tony, had point— and when it did, each let out a little more air, breath like trash as one.

Fuck, said Tony when it was gone, Fuck.

Look at that shit, said Zero, and his brother Zuchero was already picking up a handful of the new street munch. Like nothing they had ever seen before, red brick parts with shiny shards of glass.

We can do something with this.

Fuck yeah we can, those fucks can grind down our explosives for us.

It's like a tank, a smooth tank, rolling down the alley. Poor-fare moms with dry tits swilling Faygo cans of run-off, can't get any food, using dead babies like doorstops, and the city-

state can fucking afford a new smooth tank to hunt little old us. I hope to holy shit Dios-Fuego can use that shit for our bombs, said Raerae. Her face looked like it was on the verge of crying, but it always did. Regardless, she could dish out more cold torture than any of the boys. They were scared of her, and they all wanted her, and this made them even more scared.

We gonna fuck em, we gonna fuck em, we gonna blow that shit up, said Zuchero jumping up and down pouring the glass-brick powder from hand to hand. He was also squeezing it together in between his gloves like he was trying to make a snow-ball, a solid of the powder that he could throw.

Maybe, said Zero, but killer tires like that could be flame retardant.

Everything melts at some point, said Tony. Dios-Fuego knows what he is doing. The glass pieces in brick has got to do something, add a little something, a little sharp and a little weight.

The tires might just be the beginning. We don't know what else is new on those things. The windows? That could be trouble. We gotta know more. But Raerae might be right, it might be a tank, and that can work for us. Once we get *something in, what once protected the pigs from the outside only prevents them from escape. Their fortress is their tomb, said Zero.*

Their fortress is their tomb, whispered Raerae, frightfully sexy.

Zuchero was well ahead now and peeking around the corner. He tongue-clicked that the patrol car was out of sight, and they came out of the alley, reflexively kicking through trash. Nothing there they needed.

####

Dios-Fuego was in his lab when they entered, and Franco, the Shit-Supreme, was teaching kindergarten in the big room. Shit-Supreme was a title Zero bestowed on him when he had only been on the streets a month and Franco had taken in him and little Zuchero. Six years now, Zero was his sixteen-year-old right hand, and the title had spread to other groups. Every syndicate out there now had a Shit-Supreme.

Goggles and gas masks all hung from the same hooks by the door. Scarves and bandanas dried on a line close by. Zero nodded and clicked and led Raerae and Zuchero, his hands full and open like a beggar wanting to share some alms, around the seated crowd to the lab. Tony went to his bedroll and bag to get his whetstone and lied down at the edge of the room to listen and do some sharpening.

The more laws, the more outlaws. The more crimes, the more criminals. It is a simple equation. Do you children understand what an equation is? This is the one plus one equals two of what happened to your world. Your parents threw you out because there were too many rules they had to follow in raising you. Some of you wound up on the streets because your parents were arrested because it is harder to be lawful than being unlawful, said Shit-Supreme Franco, engaging each little face, some drooping, some drooling, picking their little noses and scratching their little asses.

Your parents could not resist thinking thoughts that were criminal; none of us can. Even the thought of resisting those thoughts is a crime. It is attempted crime-thought. The lucky ones are never called out on it. Shit forbid, he boomed in a loud whisper at the kids, you keep a diary or follow the damning cat of curiosity into cyber-connectivity.

Tony was a giant at fifteen, but had never known his parents and liked to listen to these parts of the lessons and wonder what it was that outlawed them before he was born. He was forcibly extracted since there was no proof he participated in utero in his parents' crimes. That is what the worker assumed at the home for pre-birth citizens who cared for him until his escape.

In the lab, Zuchero poured out on the folding table his offering of brick-glass powder and instantly started sifting swirls and circles into it.

So that is what the tires could do to bottles and bricks and what else other trash that gets in their way, Zero told Dios-Fuego.

They are stepping it up for us, said Raerae. It was still a hard-bodied cruiser, but it seemed thicker now in every way. It growled and purred at once, right down the alley.

Gerrrr, purrrr, gerrr, purrr, I don't fucking care, said Dios-Fuego, and raised his welding mask and then raised an eyebrow. What have I told you? Listen to me, I am a scientist. Everything burns, everything melts, everything booms. Everything dies if treated right. We could sing it. Everything burns, everything melts, everything booms. Everything dies if treated right. I don't worry. A man with more fingers than me worries.

He had only seven.

Worry not, precious girl, precious girl, he said stroking from her forehead down her nose with his right thumb. This one touched inside the flame, he said and holds up a short right index nub then smiles and strokes the ghost finger down the same path his thumb went.

Raerae coos.

You are anointed a priestess of sharpened hate, a burning flame of steel and derision. Baptized in piss and gasoline, your vision is forged in the ashes of every god, and what were once chains are now your teeth to tear your enemy.

He knew how to make her coo. But it seemed mutual as she described the parameters of the ghost finger with her tongue.

If I wanted sermonizing I could go out and listen to Shit-Supreme, said Zero. We brought this to you less out of fear of the new cars and more out of consideration that you, our mighty and mystically-nubbed scientist, could maybe use a ground powder of brick, glass, and street shit.

Raerae and Dios-Fuego released their holds on each other.

Yes, yes, very well, yes, Zero, that is a good idea, the scientist said. Your brother should have no trouble

collecting more. I might have just the right spices to make a
nice explosive meatball with that powder.

####

Landry stops at the end of this section. The book just rolls on like that, no chapters, just sections with four number signs after each one for over four hundred pages. He closes the book and sips from his coffee. He needs to let the book sit with him. Reading it made him feel strange. His heart rate is still mounting and he is anxious. Maybe it's the coffee, he thinks, but he has another sip anyway and slowly pushes the book a few inches farther away across the table.

In finding that name, MAAWAAM, in writing that character, a mysterious, shadowy, secondary character in a book about a quixotic fool of a protagonist from suburban Atlanta lost out in the world amidst an ancient conspiracy, MAAWAAM, a secondary character in that novel, who writes a novel in which he creates a dark and embattled apocalyptic world, a novel received with as much interest, intrigue, and controversy as the enigmatic author himself garners, a man of one name, MAAWAAM, and all the social and political implications it provokes; in finding that name, and writing that character, I was writing a role for myself. I could write the novel, *The Secret Name*, and I could stage it like I found it, a manuscript in a box somewhere, and I am just the editor of it, and the actual author is this MAAWAAM. He is the author of the inner and outer text. The story of Landry Bread just floats there in the middle. His adventures exist on a plane in between   the plane of the author of *The Secret Name*, MAAWAAM, and the author of *Amerika the Beautifuk*, MAAWAAM. The title of *Amerika the Beautifuk* is spelled in print on the book's cover but with red spray paint slashes, one turning the "c" in America into a "k," and two turning the "l" in beautiful into a "k."

Now everything is clear.
I admit my defeat. The tongue
of my ravings in my ear
is the tongue of a stranger.

I am MAAWAAM

In the 14th century, its center there about, Juan de Maawaam saw all of his glory crumble before his eyes. He had covered the known world, and some parts unknown, in pursuit of vengeance and yet found love along the way. She channeled his passion for vengeance into a passion for flesh, her flesh. So much of his fortune had been occupied in pursuit of the object of his most severe derision, chests of gold reserved for further pursuit. Now with her, his gold, as well as himself, was able to return home to Cantabria, the only Moor to settle that far north. There he settled into his castle by the sea. It was there he turned his back to everything but her. It was there his search finally ended years after he stopped searching. The past will never stay past. If you don't want it to catch up with you then you must catch up with it. Juan de Maawaam's father understood this. The pursued has no choice but to pursue the pursuer. The Viscount de Maawaam returned to his former castle and killed his own son in the early light of morning. He will be the last de Maawaam; this is what he wants to believe. His son's new bride greets him with open arms and legs. The seed of another Maawaam already stirs beneath her surface.

It helps to try the name on for size and take it out for a spin. A name makes all the difference. A name is who you are, and it/you must be pure tautology. Think of the semiotic beauty of Hanna-Barbera's Grape Ape. He was a giant grape-colored ape. His name was Grape Ape, and the only words he could say were "grape ape." He was what he said and that was his name. He was perfect.

I

AM

MAAWAAM

Goodbye Mr. Totney
Hello Mr. Tany
Thomas is no more
Only...

Thearaujohn!

Maawaam is thrice great, Maawaam Trismegistus!

NOM

DE
FUCKING
Guerre

The Words of MAAWAAM:

If you are reading this, then there is a bomb on the plane, on every plane, in your mind, right now.

We Shadow Women and Men are terrorists of the highest order. Physical violence is beneath us—unless you consider the internal world physical, and why shouldn't you, where else do the emotions lie, trauma is very real; but unlike Klans, States, and Qaedas, we have consent, humanity is entrusted to us—and we are practitioners of cultural terrorism, metaphysical terrorism, ontological terrorism, semiotic terrorism, the truest arts, the highest duty, the greatest calling...the heaviest burden.

Brother Bataille guides Maawaam more than he ever guided me. He was always there though, in the Bardo, ready to speak when I was ready to listen. He called to me first before I ever stepped out of the light. I had been up all night and felt the rising sun cut at me between the giant tombstones of the NYC skyline as I drove down the West Side Highway. Tom and Adrienne and I wandered the streets, feeling like shadows of ourselves, waiting for The Strand to open. We spun Rosenthal's Cube at Astor Place, and its impossible weight and precariousness still amused us. The city was teeming alive around us, angels sat high on the tombstones, and we felt soft and invisible in the crowd.

In the Strand we went straight to the

basement; random searching-non-searching fit our listlessness. From the darkness of a dusty bin, Brother Bataille pulled my strings with a cry of Literature and Evil. I don't know if that book followed me home or I followed it home. Into that book I returned over the years, diving, swimming, drowning.

Today, he still reminds/teaches Maawaam of so much as they meet within the Bardo and without:

Poetry alone, which denies and destroys the limitations of things, can return us to this absence of limitations—in short, the world is given to us when the image which we have within us is sacred, because all that is sacred is poetic and all that is poetic is sacred.

I have tried in my own way to be free... I have tried in my own way to give up the ghost. So many ghosts to give up before the final ghost... ghosts and angels... ghosts and angels... This is my drunken midnight choir.

When I was nineteen I finished a short story that still serves as a prime indicator of the Shadow Man I was destined to become and the insights I already had into that/this world. It is a cry of the heart in a heartless, earless world. It is a three-page hieroglyph representing both pain and secrecy. Since I was a child I have wept into a vacuum. On a year off after my first year of college, I briefly lived alone in an apartment in a town where I knew no one. This was different from the couch-surfing and kindness of friends and strangers that kept me buoyant the rest of that year. In that apartment, I had a small table and one chair, a television and VCR on the floor, a bed, and stacks of books flanking the bed. On a then-ancient laptop, an early prototype of the now-indispensible tool for the work of Shadow Men and laypersons alike, I carved out this story, a slice of my own alien heart. Years later I would show it to a professor at my college who taught a class on the short story as a literary form. He dismissed the story as not literature, but an inside joke. Maybe he was right. Here it is:

Mostly Sparrows and Jays

The night stuck to our skin at the rate of the wind, like bugs to a windshield. You don't know heartache like the look in her eyes that night; it was enough to make your tear ducts dry heave. Death rides his pale cow over the rooftops, the sour milk is on our lips. I took her hand and led her inside. Her palm was moist. So was mine.

Inside, the room spun around in square shards of light as the crystal chandelier remained still. Suddenly, a noise in the void shattered the Great Silence. She spoke.

"You're going to kill my lemur, aren't you?"

Her lemur? Oh, that primate friend of hers. The thought never crossed my mind. I intended to kill her. I began to worry. The lemur was a gift from an uncle of hers. He was a mercantile sea captain of some sort who smuggled the lemur out of Madagascar for her. Maybe the lemur was the link. I couldn't be sure and I couldn't risk the chance.

"Suzy!?! What in heaven's name are you talking about? I don't want to kill the little guy. I just want to play with little Diego."

"His name's Spanky, not Diego. I don't know why you always called him that."

"I guess he just looks like a Diego. Now where is he?"

There was a smack of air, followed by moisture, against the window as a storm came on like a snarling tempestuous dog. The house shook as if the dog wanted in. The tension returned.

"Why do you want to see Spanky, anyway? You never wanted to play with him before."

I had to think fast on my feet. Suspicion filled her eyes more than fear. I had to be quick and very smooth.

"I dig lemurs now. You say I never show interest in the stuff you like, so I did some research and I think lemurs are really cool. They're such beautiful creatures; it's a shame they are endangered." I was grabbing at straws. "I just want to give a little back to make up for what our species has taken away."

"Oh honey, that's beautiful. I never knew you felt so strongly about animals. Thank you. Spanky is going to be so excited that you want to play. I'll go get him."

She bought it. Good. I never thought it was she, but how else could they find out about me? It must be the lemur. That crazy look in his red eyes, his nocturnal habits, it all made sense now.

The walls were black in the shadow of what light? Suzy's footsteps and the scamper of the lemur could be heard above. I must find my contact man. The next meeting place is the astral plane just minutes after I fall asleep. I feel better that the girl isn't a security risk, but now I face the lemur. Dealing with a prosimian takes this conflict to a different level. A headlight or the moon, like a candle behind a pumpkin's horrific face, flashed through the window.

She came down the stairs with such joy in her eyes that it hurt so much to be a man who doesn't question orders. Knowledge is the fruit that ceases to be sweet as it stings bitten lips.

"Here you go Spanky, play with daddy," she said as she handed over the lemur.

I take the beast and we sit down at the table, him on the table, me in a chair, eye to eye, mano a mano. "Spanky, let me tell you a little story." I say with poise. Suzy goes to leave, but lingers in the doorway. The trust is questioned. The pressure is on. The moon rests on a cushion of black clouds, light, comfortable, false.

"Spanky, sometimes people have a role to play, a role they do not choose, but are given, and must play, nonetheless." He's drawn in, I've got him. "For instance, when I was a child I was given a part in my school's play. We were doing the play *The Rise and Fall of Adolf Hitler* and I was so excited about being in the play I didn't care what I had to do. They gave me one of the biggest parts. I got to play the little Jewish boy who stands in the middle of the concentration camp staring up at the sky with head cocked, saying he can hear birds singing, mostly sparrows and jays, clear and crisp and beautiful."

Shit.

I couldn't go on. The room grayed as the silty charcoal-dust of silence fell. The heaviness of the quiet held time at bay. My hand played, the move was his.

Clicking noises came from the lemur, many noises, fast and loud. No training could ever prepare. I went dizzy as his red eyes flamed. He went back on his hind legs and his ring-tail went erect. He won. I shouldn't have been chosen. The curtain is torn. There is no safety from the sun. Suzy moves in and then stops as my arms swing around Spanky's ashen neck in a tight tearful embrace. I couldn't help but cry, cry and squeeze that lemur tight. Through defeat, there is release. Suzy put her hand on my shoulder and I could feel her horror grow as mine was finally ending.

I went to hear Anne Waldman read her poetry. It was a boon for my small town to have her, but this is a college town and important people can be brought through. I have always suspected her of being a Shadow Woman, suspected that she was one of us. After she read, I approached her with her book, *Fast Speaking Woman,* for her to sign. She smiled at me. We spoke briefly. And there it is in my book, right on the title page:

"To _____, 'New Shadows, Old Shadows,' Anne Waldman."

"A word of warning: Tourists and vagabonds are the metaphors of contemporary life." (Zygmunt Bauman)

We always want to give up the ghost. Our lives, our work, it's just so lonely and hard. Brother Benjamin had his codes, as we all do. In his "Agesilaus Santander,"—a sneaky little anagram for Der Angelus Satanus—he lets on about our work, talking about angels: "new ones each moment in countless hosts, are created so that after they have sung their hymn before God, they cease to exist and pass away into nothingness." That is the way of Shadow Men and other artists.

When I read/experience the work of other Shadow Men I feel less alone. We can do that for each other.

Some of us are born in the Shadow, born out of the light, born half gone already.

The Words of MaaWaaM:

>Kill your children before they kill you.
>Kill your elders before they kill you.
>There is only now.
>There is only you.

The Words of MAaWaAM:
>You can't drown if you ARE the ocean.
>Be the ocean.

The Shadow world, our world, is a world where Ducasse is a Comte, where Kathy Acker is a pirate, where Basquiat is a Prince, where Nietzsche is Polish Royalty, Moondog a Viking, Abez a Nature Boy, and where William S. Burroughs is The Old Man of the Mountain

The Words of MaawaaM:

If when you are making your art you do not experience the terrifying giddy glee of utter abandon in freedom then you are doing it wrong.

If when you are making your love you do not experience the terrifying giddy glee of utter abandon in freedom then you are doing it wrong.

If when you are making your meal you do not experience the terrifying giddy glee of utter abandon in freedom then you are doing it wrong.

If when...   not...
                              doing it wrong.

If when...   not...
                              doing it wrong.

If when...   not...
                              doing it wrong.

There is a savior in the streets
He sleeps in the gutter and spits
A brackish wretch

Profane Illumination

The buildings sway like towering angels

Oh, Profane Illumination

Thesis → Antithesis → Synthesis

The Banal → Intoxication → Profane Illumination

The Words of MaawaaM:

> He who speaks, knows.
> He who doesn't speak, doesn't know.
> Silence is complicity.
> Silence is DEATH.

The Shadow Man is never ABOVE it all. The Shadow Man is always IN it all. Sometimes this is overwhelming, sometimes this is our death. Ecstasy, rapture, implosion, it can be too much. It is everything. The urge to run, cry, vomit, all at once, ex-stasis, to tear from one's skin. We become possessed by the spirit of the God Pan, God of Nature, God of Everything, God of Panic, for panic comes from the physical realization of the connection between all things.

But when the work, our work, is right, it is to feel at peace in ALL things. Still the tears well at the corners of my eyes, in the center of a whirl-wind/world-wind,

There is only now.

★

The Words of Maahraam:
You can't drown if you
are the ocean.

★

The Words of Maahtaam:
He who speaks, knows
He who doesn't speak
  doesn't know.
Silence is complicity.
Silence is death.

★

The shadow man is
never ABOVE it all.
The shadow man is

always IN it all.
Sometimes this is over-
whelming, sometimes
this is our death.
Ecstasy, rapture, implosion,
it can be too much. It
is everything. The urge
to run, cry, vomit all
at once, ex-stasis,
to tear from one's
skin. But when the
work is right, our
work. To feel at
peace in it ALL. Still
the tears well at
the corners of my eyes,
in the center of a
world-wind/whirlwind

when the crush from all directions stills just at the
borders of my being and there is I, and no longer an I,
just the moment, ephemeral, fleeting, there but gone.
That is when we are right. In it ALL.

"Life is a flickering shadow, with violence before and aft," Brother Burroughs.

What do other animals do all the time in the wild? They watch, watching all the time, always watching. They are reading their surroundings, reading their worlds. Not just watching, but smelling, feeling the world around them. This is our natural state, this is what the Shadow Man does.

Sister Carson once told me, "My task is to carry secret burdens for the world."

Brother Benjamin reminds us: "The reader, the thinker, the loiterer, the flaneur, are types of illuminati just as much as the opium-eater, the dreamer, the ecstatic. And more profane. Not to mention that most terrible drug—ourselves—which we take in solitude."

Many names for what we do. Totally profane. Here and now. Always here and now.

The Words of MAawaAM:

Walk every step as if you are walking to your gallows. Even if your head hangs, keep your back straight and chest full.

"I might compare her to a black sun, if you could imagine a black star pouring forth light and happiness. But she reminds you more readily of the moon, which probably branded her with her fearsome influence. Not the white moon of romance, which resembles a frigid bride, but the sinister and intoxicating moon, suspended deep within a stormy night and jostled by fleeing clouds... A stubborn will and the love of prey dwell on her brow...

"Some women inspire the need to defeat them

and take full pleasure from them; but this one arouses the desire to die slowly under her gaze."

Ah, Brother Baudelaire knew my same dark angel and tried to give up the ghost, our ghost, in the very same prose poem.

Beauty is the abyss.

"Studying the beautiful is a duel in which the artist shrieks with fright before being defeated."

The abyss is beautiful.

The Words of maaWaam:

Be so deadly serious in all that you do that it is laughable.

Never stop laughing.

The later work of Maawaam was all comprised of bomb stories. His name was big enough that he could always find an outlet—editors regularly banging on his agent's electronic door—so that every month somewhere there was published a Maawaam short story, surpassing the productivity and ubiquity of even Joyce Carol Oates, and all were bomb stories, every story telling of the lead up to, fall out from, or chaotic bloody middle of a bomb story.

Why do you write so much about bombs? I will be asked by an interviewer one day.

Because I can think of no more terrifying aspect of the modern world. Bomb is pure Otherness. It is not who we are; it is horror and it is truth.

This should go in *Bomb*, but since *Bomb* will never happen, it should go to Maawaam; he could do it justice. Like in all those absurdist modernist stories of the late 19th and early 20th centuries, it is a story of a man who wakes up to find a bomb strapped to his chest. He freaks out, goes to the police, they can't get it off, the bomber sends a message, the man is made to do various tasks under threat, eventually the bomber stops communicating, the police have a wait-and-see approach. Days become weeks, become months, become years, all with bomb on. He eats, showers, sleeps with bomb. Eventually he tries dating. It isn't so weird, everyone knows him from the news, he has a level of celebrity. At first he instills fear, then novelty and attraction, then eventually he is common-place, with a bit of backlash, people are upset he hasn't blown up yet. He is spectacle, but more so spectacle of potential. The longer it goes, the more used to the bomb he gets, the more agitated the public gets that he hasn't fulfilled what they want: They want to see him explode. I'm not sure how it should end. Public kills him, or he blows himself up to please others, or he grows old and dies of cancer and the bomb comes off, too old to work, the bomber's name is inside, he has been long dead they find out.

Maawaam will know how it should end.

Erotic Agony

Deep Painful Joy

The Words of mAawaAm:

"Plagiarism is the most atrocious literary crime." Even though I take full credit for that statement, I am sure you can think of something worse. I know we are both thinking of something worse right now. Can you see it? Can you feel it? DO NOT SAY IT.

Maawaam was born in May of 1871, during the teeming thickness of the Paris Commune. The fierce lady-Communard who bore him gave him up to a Roma gypsy. It was she who named him, she who took him in and raised him in the gypsy ways. She gave him a name that could protect him from all directions. A name of teeth-points that could rotate around an axis. It was a name he would grow into in hushed alleys and catacombs. Soot-browned, little Maawaam would draw coins and purses from training dummies with no alarm bell ringing down amongst the bones of crusaders under the city. They told him the story of "The Boy Whose Heart Was a Ticking Bomb." The boy's mother was the victim of the gypsy curse. Soon after the curse was applied, the hapless mother referred to her child as "an infernal machine," and "may you have everything your ask for" came true for her: Her child became an infernal machine.

I sit back and put on Maawaam. I feel our way into our skin. I read Lindqvist's *History of Bombing* and some of Maawaam's stories come to life before my eyes.

Maawaam gives these story ideas to the world to finish for him. One collective consciousness, storying together.

Words of maawaam:

Burn every bridge behind you. Burn every bridge before you.

There is no past. There is no future.

Burn every bridge beneath you.

Relax

Fall.

Maawaam has become this Shadow Man's shadow. He is the ghost in this machine.

Maawaam saw so much sadness in the world, all he ever wanted to do was help people.

I have been writing suicide notes since I was thirteen. I prefer to leave them out in the open, to be found, found on my watch. They are not secrets, they are poems that become real.

Every Shadow Man will forever deny being a Shadow Man.

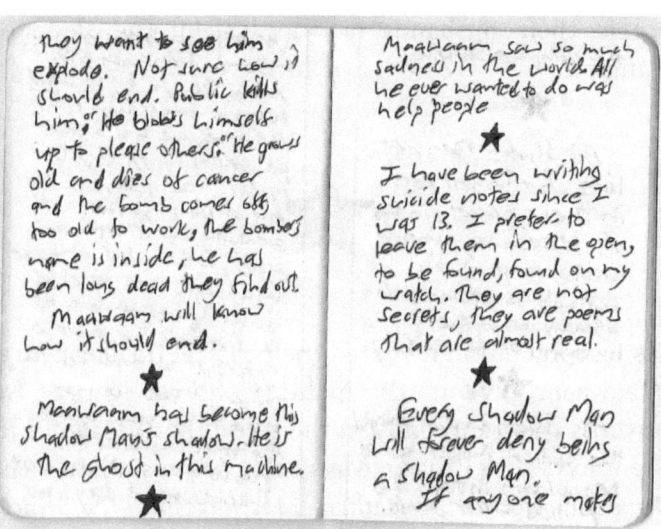

If anyone makes the claim, he is lying.

All Shadow Wo/Men are liars. The honest are in their graves, in front of televisions, punching clocks, masturbating apathetically to internet pornography

while their husbands or wives sleep the sleep of
Ambien.

As Joseph Conrad invented the political thriller genre,
Maawaam invents the political horror genre. He
invents this genre only in the sense that he names it.
He knows that it has always been with us. Plato's *The
Republic*, Hobbes' *Leviathan*, Machiavelli's *The Prince*,
Orwell's *1984*.

"The barbarian invasion is, however, necessary; it is
through this that values can regain their equilibrium:
the true reaffirmation of equal stature for the
components of a culture." (Édouard Glissant)

Words of MAawaAM:

You are the perfect crime.

All Shadow Men feel alone all the time.
No matter that we know that we are not.

Hobbes is a violent destruction of Aristotelian politics. He proposed "the individual" in the darkest way. But aren't we all born from darkness? Every person under the sun, every person of the sun. Born from darkness.

I carried much...
    I suffered much...
    Oh, multa tuli...
    Oh Multatuli...
    You were a Shadow Man, and you worked with one of our greatest tools...
    a hate, a deep profound loving and honorable hate...

There is a darkness that only Maawaam knows. A darkness that hovers around the forgotten. A darkness that once experienced is to be coveted and to be wielded at the world. There is a power in being forgotten, a power in being invisible to the majority of humans on the planet and it didn't take him long to learn it. After sorrow there was release and after release the feeling of infinite expansion.

Within the head of Maawaam, I too am free. In any time and any place I can go with the beggars and the low. I can con my way up into the highest orders of humanity. Prod princes with a ticklish tongue into investments good for all but them. Prod princesses deeply with that same silver tongue for the good of all over me. I wear Maawaam and I am free. Within that frame I can do anything and be anyone.

"In the footnotes, however (which seem like another book compulsively writing itself), we begin to see the night-side of the half-hidden face of history."

The words are following a destiny that I'm participating in. I am accepting them and carrying them forward.

The only way to make iconoclasm work is success.

If only map were territory. I'd fold the world in a way to get you to spill down where I want you. If only clocks were time, I'd spin the world back until you were naked, vulnerable, and mine.

As a teenager, Maawaam experimented with suicide notes as a prose style. He would leave them in visible places for strangers to find, strangers at malls, guidance counselors at school, dinner guests at family functions. He would hide off to the side and watch the unbeknownst reader's reaction to the note. They were all letters to a friend he didn't have.

Dear Friend,

Life only works
If everyone always
       lies
All the time.

I'll miss you,
I'm an honest man.
Dear Friend...

Dear Friend,

I keep failing the
        test of days
But a day that never
        starts can
        never end.

Remember this,
Dear Friend...

The spy brings into the real world, a treacherous world, the skills, the craft of the actor, the novelist, the poet. To create fictions, narratives, stories for and in life-or-death situations is what they do, often off the cuff, on the fly. Same for con men, grifters, some criminals. They are also all readers, reading the world, people, situations, clocking every game.

Far, or forgot, to me is near;
    Shadow and sunlight are
    the same;

The vanished gods to me appear;
    And one to me are
    Shame and fame.

"I will make my scaffold of a stage," Tripmaster Monkey.

The next book that Maawaam will write will be called, *Yes Virginia, Jet Fuel Can't Melt Steel Beams*. Reviews will call it *The Necronomicon* for our time. It will be a furious fever dream of paranoia, deep truths, historical double-crosses, future predictions, and rare violence. The act of reading it will induce nausea, anxiety, discomfort, rashes, itching, erections, vomiting, lose stool, anal leakage, insomnia, rage, depression, opposition to authority, listlessness, sheepishness, sheeplessness, night terrors, obsessive compulsions, fear of the dark, sexual reorientation, and in some, madness, complete pituitary shutdown, death, and religious devotion to shows of strength. To read the book will be a crime. To not read the book will also be a crime. The book will make everyone a criminal. It will be banned in the US, Euro Zone, and countries receiving western aid; e-book downloads will be flagged by NSA and Homeland Security as well as any mention of it in correspondence in email, text messages, and phone calls. It will lurk in the deep web, but it will live in print, on paper, transported and read by hand by those that care about the freedom of expression and the sovereignty of the artist to live in that artist's own world by the code of the assassin, as dictated by the Old Man of the Mountain himself, Hassan i Sabbah: *Nothing Is True, Everything Is Permitted.*

A book is forever air-gapped. A book is free from surveillance, corruption, and culpability.

We've acknowledged that the only constant is change; relaxed into it, even.
What it means though is that no one or thing is to be trusted.
Each Other is a shimmering haze of atoms.
No one is solid, nothing is true.

When you're a spy everything you go through is private. Every pain is yours alone. After enough time deep cover you can channel a pain or sorrow and maybe express it as something else, or even a pain or sorrow as long as you put it on something else. You, the true you, the other you, can never be seen or never seen in a way that anyone knows what they're seeing. Of course, everything they see is you. It's all you, in sum and shadow. You are Plato's Cave; you project what shadows you need. But your pain is your own. An emotional wound is worse than physical; it is there that the corruption seeps in. At first it is a salve—compassion, fellow feeling, humanity—but it is here you betray yourself to yourself. You have to be human. People need to see that. Humanity is your cover. You gotta smile, but you also have to cry, at a puppy, at a kindness, a sadness. Give 'em the range. Paint deception with all the colors of the heart.

As Maawaam I can tell the story and be the story. Here's another Words of Maawaam:

> Every story is best told
> In first person

On the first day I created the heavens and the earth.

On November 3, 1957, I put a dog named Laika into a rocket named Sputnik and shot it into space. Laika, the happiest and sweetest street dog of the three, died within hours of launch.

It was the first time the Kabbalist had worked on English but the numbers, they were so clear. They took him away from his discipline into a brand new terrain.

13-1-1-23-1-1-13

They were perfect.
The value of twenty-three flanked on both sides by the value of fifteen.
The holy fool starts from home at the 13th letter on a journey and climbs down to the 1st letter, the origin, and he circles it, threading back through the 1st letter again before the steepest of climbs to the peak of heavenly chaos at the 23rd letter and then back down twice through the chthonic abyss of the 1st again and again to return home to his place in the 13th.

There is only one divination now.

I need her to know Maawaam.

But how could she not fear him.

I fear him myself.

I want her to love me, to love Maawaam, to love me, to love Maawaam, and I don't want to bear this burden alone, to bear Maawaam alone, and it is her, it is she who can hear the sounds of summer just beyond the window, she who loves the poet in me, she who tries to tease the ghost out from within me, she, she, she, a partner, a girlfriend, a radiant goddess, a wife, maybe...

...And in the Bardo, through the modulations of Sister Carson, I hear-feel-embrace the words of Sister Sappho for my time, the truth of love and duty:

> *Come to me now: loose me from hard*
> *care and all my heart longs*
> *to accomplish, accomplish. You*
> *be my ally.*

It is through Maawaam that I can walk in the light.

It is said that on his deathbed Balzac called out for some of his characters by name.

Cantabria, 33000 BCE

Maawaam trudges up over the icy roll of hillock, her pelt boot crunching through to hints of green below. She has left the group to practice what she will teach them tomorrow. Her name is a soft-mouthed grunt to them. To speak her comforts them. They have no idea how much she does for them. She came from elsewhere but she knew them, she cared for them.

Over the ridge she found the entrance to the cave, and just within its opening, a wide domed space. Her staff was already wrapped with pitch at it's top and the bottom was sharpened on her walk, ready to stab into the damp earth. From the folded pelts tied to her back she drew a hefty rock of hematite, glinting like a black star in the new light of her torch. In her dreams her purpose and practice had become clear and rehearsed. Now with the cave walls and ceilings bright before her, she set to work. In this womb of earth she planted seeds, various seeds to various purposes. These seeds of thought, the thought of bison will gestate. Growing in this womb it will be birth a thousand times upon the surface. It will stamp down the ice, cracking it with herds of hoofs and the green beneath will rise and run wide with the herd.

Tomorrow she will lead them here, and tomorrow she will teach them to draw with charcoal from the beneath the flames and the rocks that they can mine. Bison and deer will be shaped and planted in the earth as the power to draw is planted in each of the people. Across curves in the cave ceiling the animals will burst forth with added dimension, but that lesson will come later. They will sign their work with their hands, its print a portrait of selfhood and capability. They will mumble, growl, and weep the name Maawaam after she is gone and forgotten. Her name will vibrate in their breath and flow through all their creations.

Editor's Acknowledgements:

There are many people who I would like to thank in making this work of literary scholarship possible: my wife Jessica, for always being there, even when I wasn't; Fox Marlowe, for existing; Dad and Jody; Ariane, Clint, John, and Catherine; Jonathan, Emily, Ada, and Gail Polk; Tiffany and Elijah Chameides; Tanya, Andy, and Cecilie Frazee; Matt and Shawn McKinney; Travis and Susie Burch; West Price; Neil Graff; Micheal Karczewski; Michael Petri and Tara Biamby; Brian and Anna Grace; Liz Cunningham; William, Crystal, Quentin, and Greyson Brandon; Kai Reidl; Amy and Adrienne Gandolfi; Melissa Leahy; Nathan Koldys; Lazarus Roth; Molly Williams; James Treadway. And where would I be without Mark Hewitt (for friendship and proofreading)?

I would like to take this chance in the Editor's Acknowledgements to dedicate this book to the memory of Dr. Kenneth Pittman. His Politics and Literature class along with his presence and brief mentorship helped me to look at the world and my actions in it in a new and different way. An ever-eager student, I've had lots of teachers and mentors who have left their mark on me and all the works I touch: Peter Gardella, Van Hartmann, Carolyn Medine, Glenn

Wallis, Joel Black, Peter O'Neill, Thomas Cerbu, Reginald McKnight, and William T. Vollmann.

Nate Ragolia and Shaunn Grulkowski of Spaceboy Books, you guys are the real heroes for publishing such a strange artifact of humanity's greatest secret. T.J. Stambaugh, thank you for the wonderful work here in helping curate some of Maawaam's art. Dan Pecci was very helpful in finding the cover of Maawaam's book.

And to those who have departed recently, Daniel Chameides, Curtis Vorda, Jeremy Ayers, and Raymond Langley, I think you all would have loved Maawaam. I'll tell you all about him on the next bardo.

About the Editor

Jordan A. Rothacker is a poet, novelist, and essayist living in Athens, Georgia where he earned a Masters in Religion and a PhD in Comparative Literature at the University of Georgia. Rothacker majored in Philosophy at Manhattanville College in Purchase, New York and his life has been split between Georgia and New York (where he was born); he dreams of going west. His journalism has appeared in periodicals as diverse as *Vegetarian Times* and *International Wristwatch*, while his fiction, poetry, reviews, and essays can be found in such illustrious venues as *Red River Review, Dark Matter, Dead Flowers, Stone Highway Review, May Day, As It Ought to Be, The Exquisite Corpse, The Believer, Bomb Magazine*, and *Guernica*. For book length work check out Rothacker's *The Pit, and No Other Stories* (Black Hill Press 2015), a novella (or "micro-epic" as he calls it) and his first full-length novel, *And Wind Will Wash Away* (Deeds Publishing, 2016). His fiction can also be found in *The Cost of Paper: II* (2015), *The Cost of Paper: III* (2016), and *The Cost of Paper: IV* (2017), anthologies from Black Hill Press edited by William M. Brandon III. He loves sandwiches (a category in which he classifies pizza and tacos) and debating taxonomy almost as much as he loves his wife, his son, his dogs, and his cat, Whiskey.

For more information see jordanrothacker.com

About the Publishing Team

TJ Stambaugh received several commendations for his bravery as a battalion commander in the Meme Wars. After the war, TJ retired to Catonsville, MD, where he paints, enjoys movies you have to read, and is Art Director for Spaceboy Books LLC.

Nate Ragolia is a lifelong lover of science fiction, and a nerd/geek. In 2015, his first book, *There You Feel Free* was published by 1888's Black Hill Press. In 2017, his second book, *The Retroactivist*, was published by Spaceboy Books LLC. He founded *BONED: A Collection of Skeletal Writings*. He also writes articles on Medium, and dabbles in fiction, poetry, and screenplays.

Amanda Hardebeck has been a sci-fi & film addict since birth. When her older brother handed her a copy of *Dune* for her birthday 20 years ago, her passion for science fiction took off. She is a roller derby referee for her hometown team and is Chief Editor for Spaceboy Books LLC.

Learn more about Spaceboy Books online at: readspaceboy.com